KISSANDRA SMITH

THE REBELLION
of
MARY MAGDALENE

ᐸAMERHOGNE
PRESS

Kissandra Smith

ISBN: 9781729295427

Cover design and layout by Bassanio Graneau

Acknowledgements

Kindness is not rare. A hearty thank you to Isatou Jallow, Shane Mc Quilkin and Bassanio Graneau, although words cannot suffice.

To Mme Nour Ikken Bennis
With the deepest love and respect
I thank you for every word of encouragement,
every good advice and every bit of kindness.
To Morocco and all her beautiful people; her sweet spices,
captivating landscape and rich memories...
Vive le Maroc!

CONTENTS

THE REBELLION

of

MARY MAGDALENE

Everyone has a story. Even the man writing the story has a story and man is made up of chapters, hidden themes, similes, ironies and metaphors. In the end, grammar and good conjunctions are always the victor.

Dear Mary,

May the one who grants, grant you all that is beautiful in this world and the next. May he free you from oppression. May he lead you not into the temptation of being an oppressor, for vile is the act.

May he rectify your affairs and may he give you a beautiful paradise befitting a Mary—and a Mary is one who brings revolution and justice to the world. Easy is it to fight for your own self, but more courageous is it to fight for others.

Burn us at the stake, throw us in the gallows and we shall be reborn only to be the phoenix. Viva la Mary! Viva la revolución.

Sincerest love
Ole Mary

A poet once looked to the stars, and she asked, "Dear stars, why do you continue to shine, when you are encompassed by darkness and your only hope is round?"

The stars said to the poet, "We look not unto the world with eyes that were bestowed unto us, but instead we look at the world with the eyes of a child and so we only see innocence and beauty, thus our light. And also, there are many to whom our light has brought great joy. So despite our predicament we continue to shine."

1.

A Child's Eyes

The creaking sound from the shutting of the wooden mustard-yellow door as we made our departure for school, was often mixed with my mother's voice, warning us to return home early or face her wrath—and mother's wrath was indeed the wrath.

My mother had the ability to transform anything into a punishing device—the old ugly pots, the born-again wooden pot-spoon, the cream bamboo broom which had lost many of its thin teeth over the years, the big grater she used for grating coconut on some mornings—whose soul had lost its vigour and shine, her two pairs of worn out black shoes. Sometimes even the books she kept on the shelf, would conspire with her to keep us in line.

I remember one day in particular she gave me a scolding with her old prayer book. I had surrendered to an urge to pinch off piece of the freshly baked vanilla and chocolate cake she had just removed from the outside oven. The cake's enticing aroma had seduced me to a brief state of madness. I recall being in a forever state of deep contemplation, before my body floated to the kitchen counter where the cake was left for cooling, and my index finger and thumb went in for the prize—the sweet rich taste of the cake sang melodiously to each one of my taste buds. I also vividly remember thinking this day was indeed my last on God's earth, as my mother unleashed prayer after prayer from the hardcover and brittle pages of the prayer book over my body. Mother's wrath was indeed the wrath.

However, in spite of all the castigating we were loved dearly by our mother. It was evident in the way she said goodbye, religiously kissing our faces before we left for school or greeting us with a smile when we returned home. Her affection was subliminally expressed in the way she prepared the rich golden corn flour porridge for breakfast, bathed in nourishing coconut milk mixed with spice and bayleaf and finely grated ginger—sometimes with a fresh slice of papaya or orange on the side or some other fruit.

Her love was also shown in the way she kept us clean all the time. She would scour us raw with a luffa picked from the back of the house. It felt as if layers of skin were being removed from our backs and bare bottoms by the brittle fibres, as her hand armed with the luffa moved quickly over our bodies. Thereafter she would slowly rinse us, throwing water each and every way to ensure we were properly cleaned. The smell of carbolic soap or black soap and even blue soap, would linger on our bodies as proof—indeed we were loved.

The Rebellion of Mary Magdalene

My life at that time seemed ordinary, but looking back at my childhood I can say that it was far from common. Our father had died suddenly and despite Dr. Thomas's professional conclusion, that the cause of death was heart failure, the neighbours were convinced it was due to something else—'Obeah'.

Growing up I chose to believe the latter, that Obeah was indeed the cause of my father's death; mainly because it was a more convenient explanation for my already indoctrinated friends at school. Everything was Obeah and Obeah was everything growing up on the small island of Grenada.

When Soniel, the shopkeeper's son drowned in the river, people said it was Obeah—that his own father had sold him to the devil in return for riches. They all blatantly neglected the fact that Mr. Singh laboured night and day, tirelessly to make his earnings. They also omitted the fact that Soniel simply could not swim and sporadically suffered from seizures. In an attempt to prove to his peers he had no fear of the water, he took the brave and stupid plunge which ended his life.

When Miss Murl's pregnancies, all seven of them miscarried—people said it was Obeah. 'A spell on her womb' they said, 'a deed of her own mother's doing due to an ongoing land dispute' they claimed.

When Johnny Brown's left foot grew to the size of a large watermelon—he said it was Obeah due to 'all the lands' his father had left him. On early mornings, around the time the many fowls began singing and late in the evenings when they went to bed, he would be seen bathing himself in the 'river mouth' — the place where the river met the sea, as instructed by his grandmother. On his deathbed he refused medicine and remained convinced it was his brother's doing, even when Dr. Thomas insisted it was heart related. 'Water could not wash' his brother after that and so he was forced to move to Trinidad with his family.

When Jimmy, who sat in the front row just beneath the teacher's nose, one day fell down and started foaming at the mouth, then suddenly rose and drifted all the way back to his house in what appeared as a drunken state — his mother said it was Obeah. She claimed someone had 'put something' in his Royal Readers because he was the top performer in his class.

When Miss Martha's cane field burned to the ground — she said it was Obeah. Everyone knew it was of her own negligence, due to the candle she left lighting in her small hut in the middle of her cane field. "Obeah, they wicked too much! They envy me! Obeah and I know who do it! Obeah shall be returned on to you! Obeah!" she screamed, as the vermilion villain prowled from cane bed to cane bed, devouring stalk by stalk, laughing and crackling like an old hag as it destroyed a legacy that men and women alike had toiled over; once massa's land, but acquired by the children of slaves over the years.

Obeah was everything and everything was Obeah growing up in Grenada. Underneath their clothing people often wore charms and trinkets made by themselves, or by some 'Obeah man' or 'Obeah woman', or some grandmother for protection or good luck. They even drank various herbal concoctions to ward off Obeah. However, despite the heavy 'Obeah-air' which presided over the little island of Grenada, it was still a 'hush hush', a thing not publicly discussed. The practice of such a thing was often frowned upon. It was seen as retrograde and anything but modern, 'a shameful inheritance from our African ancestors'. The practice of African religions and spirituality was seen as uncivilized. Above all, it was seen as an outright disrespect to God and his manifestation in the church.

"One cannot serve two masters," the white priest said. "God is a jealous God," the white priest said, and we all nodded in church, even those wearing charms and trinkets carefully concealed below their clothing.

•••

I remember little of my father, except for the pungent smell of alcohol on his person, and the constant quarrelling between him and my mother. The quarrels were mostly about the money he had spent in the rum shop; my mother's hard earned dollars she had carefully concealed in some secret place, or so she thought on numerous occasions.

Sometimes she hid it in slits of the beddings. Sometimes she hid it in her shoes. Sometimes she hid it between the wares, the little that we had; even between the bunches of green bananas that remained neatly packed on the side of the verandah.

One time, I stood in the bedroom window watching her dig a hole in the shade of the big breadfruit tree behind the house. I saw her carefully pull the dollar bills from her bosom and place them in what I suspected was a covered tin can. She had just received her 'susu hand' after months of labouring, paying and waiting. We knew she wanted to buy an elegant piece of material, to outmatch the tired beaten-up dresses that she owned. She also promised to make us dresses too. However, it was as if the money had a voice that beckoned to my father from their hiding places—as if the money had a particular odour he could sniff out.

Sometimes that was the only money we had for food and when he was done spending it in the rum shop on himself and his friends, he would stumble into the house at odd hours saying, "Tomorrow I will do better. I will not drink the devil's juice again. I will be a good man and I will provide." His slender index finger would bob wearily, as his heavy eyes and staggering frame searched out anything to keep him upright. "I ent going to touch the money or rum again," he would continue. "I swear on my mudda head and my fadda head. I will be like my brother, the smart one, the doctor in Chaguanas—my mother's favourite," and on and on he would mope, about how he was never loved as a child and about how his mother had favoured his brother over him.

The Rebellion of Mary Magdalene

He would then drown himself in a puddle of dejection and soon after, pitiful sobs would follow as we looked on. Instinctively, I often wanted to hug him, but I knew better than to intervene. The look on my mother's face was always the same, as if she was looking at her worst enemy, an enemy whose presence tainted the very air she was breathing. A look of utmost disgust.

One night he came home and fell at her feet, touching and kissing her ankles as he repeated the same lines saying, "You used to believe in me. You used to believe in me." My mother stood there, aloof, looking down at him with familiar repugnance, until he fell asleep at her ankles—as the stench of the alcohol slowly seeped from his pores to embrace us.

We never knew what he did in the day with his time, but on most nights, the man notorious for drinking the most alcohol in our village, would stagger home to us and in the morning he would be gone. My mother referred to him as 'that man' and so we all called him 'that man'. He was never directly referred to as father, 'that man' was his name in our house. I cannot recall him ever being part of our lives or talking to us directly, offering us advice when needed, or simply showing us affection. I cannot even recall the colour of his eyes. He was a complete stranger in our home. He was 'that man'.

At his funeral, my mother made us all wear yellow—a yellow as bold as the petals from the poui tree.

She said, "Darkness has been removed from our lives and we should celebrate it."

I stood there in my bright yellow dress, trying hard to read the faces of the three other persons who were present at my father's burial; the two men my father drank rum with, and Ole Mary.

The two men wore sad masks on their youthful rumpled faces—a consequence of their undying romance with alcohol. There was Paulo who was nicknamed 'Fowl', since he made a habit of crowing early in the morning on his way home from the rum shop sometimes. After the death of his wife, the rum shop became his second home. His wife had died whilst giving birth. The baby had died also. The very umbilical cord that linked him to his mother, giving him life, had betrayed him in the end by wrapping itself adamantly around his neck. He was to be named John. They buried mother and son together.

The image of the funeral remains in my mind even today. A sleeping beauty, with skin as dark and flawless as the night itself, with an oval face and high cheekbones and long eyelashes that jutted out elegantly; a beautiful sleeping woman attired in a pearly white dress; her thick black hair beautifully adorned with a flowery bed; and her baby dressed in a royal blue jumper with a white hat on his tiny head, resting peacefully on her bosom.

I can still hear Paulo's screams echoing in my mind. Wails insync with each spade of dirt that hit the shiny brown mahogany coffin. The person whom he had known since he was fourteen years old was taken from him in the wink of an eye. The person who brought him unimaginable joy was being laid to rest at the tender age of twenty-two. This was not the growing old dream he had seen in their future. If life was a person he would have certainly strangled her with his bare hands on that day, for she had robbed him of his beloved, his pillar of sanity, in a world of poverty and despair and no way out—except through love, as love has the ability to transform the most hideous of circumstances, to a beautiful and liveable one.

Then there was 'Iron bull', who got his nickname from his strong athletic build. His second home was also the rum shop. His story was one of infidelity on his wife's part. Her name was Loraine. Loraine was a case of 'when you are in good house, bad house calls to you'. She lived in the house adjacent to ours with her 'new man'. Sometimes we would hear her bawling as blows landed on her back and on many occasions, I would see her walking the street with her head almost touching the ground, trying hard to conceal the obvious discolouration of her face. My mother was the only neighbour who intervened during some instances.

Whenever Loraine's screams grew intolerable, my mother would go to the window and call out, "Joe, monkey knows which tree to climb! Why you ent come across here and start hitting me?" On and on my mother would continue cursing Joe. I guess that was her stratagem to get Joe to stop hitting Lorraine and it always worked.

One afternoon I came home from school and found Loraine sitting on the old rocking chair in the kitchen. The old chair rocked slowly back and forth to match the melancholy disposition of the room. Even the light that peered through the kitchen window was dull, gloomy and sad. Loraine was a light- skinned woman but on that day she was black and purple from bruises and swellings. My mother was busy coaxing her to leave Joe and reconcile with her husband.

"Loraine look at you face," my mother pointed out enraged, while holding a broken piece of mirror up to Loraine's face. "You want to die? Is kill Joe going to kill you! He doesn't love you. A man that loves you will never beat you black and blue. Everyone makes mistakes. Go back to your husband. Go back to the man who treated you with love and respect. I know men like Joe. I lost two friends to men like Joe. Men like Joe are weak and will do anything to feel powerful. Is either they get into your mind and make you feel unworthy of anything good, or they will kill you and it seems as if Joe wants to kill you."

Loraine just sat there, looking into the mirror in pale silence. Tears flowed from her eyes, leaving wet blots where they had fallen on her green cotton dress. A feeling of pity and anger overcame me as my non-adolescent eyes peered through the little hole in the kitchen door — Loraine's hand trembling uncontrollably, her posture hunched over as if broken and my mother's two hands, gripping onto Loraine's shoulder while kneeling in front of her lap.

The Rebellion of Mary Magdalene

That same night, Joe came banging on our door. "Loraine you in there? I know you in there!" he shouted.

My mother yanked open the front door of our house with vexation scribbled all over her face, as she stood face to face with Joe the 'woman beater'. Her face was just inches away from his and she said, "If Loraine here, what are you going to do about it?" Joe quietly and quickly bowed his head and walked away not uttering a single word.

As I scanned the faces of the three who stood before my father's coffin, I could not help but wonder about the presence of Ole Mary—the one person who was most rarely seen in public. However, before I could formulate any assumptions, she disappeared into the bushes without uttering a single word. She had stood there dressed in a flowing white dress, her head neatly wrapped in the same fabric, her face painted with a light algae-green mud mask. She stood there staring at the coffin, murmuring something that was too low to be heard by my suddenly large ears, which were trying hard to hear what she was saying. Her eyes were filled with tears—a watery bed.

My father's coffin was made from used salt fish boxes, that my mother collected from the wharf. He laid there in his coffin wearing the suit he had worn on the day he married my mother. I remembered the suit from an old photo I had seen in my mother's suitcase. In the photo they both seemed so contented, beatific smiles on their youthful faces. My father towered over my mother, his hand possessively but lovingly resting on her shoulder while her white dress confessed a version of enchantment and fairy-tale love. In her hands, she held a resplendent bouquet of natural flowers. My father wore his white jacket that neatly complimented his dark slim physique. His beard was neatly trimmed which gave him an aristocratic demeanour.

However, on the day of his funeral, that same white jacket clung to his sober lifeless body and the seams appeared as if they were about to burst. I could not see the lower part of his body but I imagined the pants were just as tight. Over the years he had grown fat in the midsection and other parts of his body, as Mr. Williams the 'burial man' had explained. A miracle was needed for my father to look presentable in his suit, he had further stated, but my mother insisted he was to be buried in that suit and no other. She had looked Mr. Williams straight in the eyes with a menacing stare, terrifying and piercing and commanded "Well make the miracle happen. I see you all the time praying the hardest in church, so pray and he best be in that suit and no other when he is to be put in the ground."

His nicer suits, she gave away to the tailor and refused to take money for them, although we were in dire need of the money. His fancy shoes were buried in the back of the house. When asked why, my mother responded, "Those are footsteps one should never walk in." We understood clearly what she meant to convey. There was no customary happy hour after the burial.

On the day my father died, after Mr. Williams and his son came for his body with their carriage, my mother seemed more energized and undismayed more so than ever. She threw away the old photos from their wedding day. We did not cry and neither did she. It was as if he never existed, as a small cube of ice made to face the scorching sun. She gathered us all together that night and made us promise, that we would never marry for love and her words exact were, "love only brings heartache".

Later that night while lying on 'my side' of the shared bed, I wondered about my grandparents. They were rarely mentioned and whenever curiosity had led us to inquire, we were always ignored. My mother's face would suddenly take on a gloomy stare and my father would stare off into the distance as if in a trance.

···

I saw my father in a dream on the same night he was buried. He was smiling and dressed in all white. He looked slimmer and younger—the tired wrinkles from his forehead were all gone. The swelling of his cheeks and lips that came from years of sucking on rum bottles were no more. His soft black-grey hair was neatly parted in the middle. He did not speak but indicated with his hands to follow him as he ran ahead. I remember running after him and suddenly out of nowhere appeared the woman at the funeral, Ole Mary. She was dressed in her customary all white and her face was covered in the mud mask she always wore.

In the dream she carried a blue pouch. It swung from her right side and from it she removed a small brown calabash, with carved symbols on its outer surface. She walked slowly towards me. She then dipped into the calabash and withdrew her hands slowly, only to blow a white powder into my face.

The following night I had another dream. I saw a white woman dressed in a moth black dress. Her face was hidden by a halfway veil. She then suddenly transformed into a large black dog, with vicious silver fangs and a white spot planted in the middle of its forehead. The dog then transformed in to a huge black snake. It hissed at me with anger. In the dream I was screaming but no sound escaped my mouth—my voice was nowhere to be found, dried up like a desert. I was pursued for what seemed like hours by the dog but then just as it was very close to me, Ole Mary appeared and killed it, and again she blew the white powder in to my face. I woke up panting and dripping with sweat just like the night before, confused even more.

When I told my mother about the dreams, she made a paste with garlic, lime, rosemary leaves and some other unknown herbs and rubbed it all over my body the following night. She then instructed me to wear my sleeping clothes inside out. I was also told that under no circumstances, was I to reveal my dreams to anyone, not even my siblings.

In the heart, you will find a doorway to the soul. Be gentle when you knock on the door. I warn you, be gentle, be kind, because behind that door lives a beautiful soul.

2.

Broken Heart

Our house was a little green house that sat silently in a somewhat deserted part in the parish of St. David. Apart from school, our daily lives were filled with walking the distance for drinking water and our nights were painted by kerosene lamps and thrilling stories, of the mythical creatures of the dark; *loupgarou, la Diablesse* and jumbies.

As a young girl stand pipes and water taps in most houses were a dream, a luxurious one. Instead we had borehole water and river water at our disposal and of course that meant repetitious trips to their various locations. Some were within short distances, some within long and tiresome distances that left the soles of our feet sore. It was quite normal to see people carrying pails of water on their heads—a piece of cloth tucked neatly beneath, to alleviate the pain inflicted by the weight of their precious cargo. As the youngest, carrying water was not much of a task. I was always given the smallest can to carry water. Nevertheless, along the way we took our play time.

There were two things that were routine for us. One was the famous 'donkey ride' as we called it. We would divert through short cuts, intentionally looking for a donkey to steal a ride on. I can vividly recall the day a mischievous donkey threw me off its back, fracturing my left hand as a result. We then fabricated a story for our mother. I told her I had slipped and fell on the road.

The other thing we enjoyed doing was 'fruit pillaging'. It was 'thiefing' as my mom called it, but to us it was pure innocent amusement and the juicy reward of filled bellies. One sunny day in particular, we ventured into Mr. Langaigne's garden to steal his melons, as we often did, but this time we were greeted by his ferocious dogs. They were normally tied at the side of his house a safe distance away. I reckoned he had grown tired of our pillaging. Luckily we managed to outrun the dogs. They seemed contented with just chasing us off their owner's property. We laughed heartily as we ate the single juicy, sweet, ruby-red melon my brother had refused to drop during our flight from the dogs.

The stories we recounted for tarrying were always calculated with innocent adventures—having to divert off route as a result of an unforeseen occurrence or needing a rest. On the occasions when my mother asked me to confirm the stories given by the others, I was always ready after being prepped by my older siblings. I was natural at it and with a straight face I would start giving a detailed account of a dog or a cow or something. Looking back I do not think she believed my tales, but she kept quiet for some reason.

The community we lived in was very close knit. Everyone knew everyone and took care of each other. It was normal to see children running between houses to borrow rice or sugar, or to fulfil some other human need. "Mammy say send some sugar for her," was as normal as a mosquito's sonnet. The spirit of the community was evident, as cooking and inviting neighbours to join in was almost expected.

Villagers needed no reason to hold events such as *Saraca*, where a variety of foods were contributed by different persons to be shared by all—golden yellow coucou mixed with pumpkin and okra; fried Barracuda served with callaloo at the side; cow skin boiled soft and soaked in a concoction of onions, salt, peppers and various backyard seasonings; fireside steamed breadfruit and white yams, with corned fish; porridge made from the tannia plant; coconut bakes baked in makeshift ovens; conke wrapped in fig leaves; coconut sugar cakes, sweet potato pudding, coconut fudge, ginger beer, lime juice, sorrel—the food options were plentiful and very much Grenadian and very much delicious.

The adults would engage in games of dominoes, cards and retelling of events, while keeping watchful eyes on us as we took part in innocent games of hopscotch, skipping, tag and many more. Sometimes both adults and children would partake in the famous maypole dancing and limbo dance, as drums set the tone for the energetic atmosphere. It was amazing to see the older men and women compete with each other, to see who was the most flexible.

In those days, every adult was a parent and thus our upbringing was a communal one. A complete stranger once caught my sister and me 'red-handed', in the act of repeating swear words we had overheard while passing by a popular 'rum shop'. We received a scolding and a beating with a whip plucked from a nearby tamarind tree. We humbly took our punishment in bowed silence, for we knew better than to be defiant. Every adult was a parent.

Our closest neighbours were Loraine and her abusive boyfriend. Loraine eventually reconciled with her husband Iron Bull and moved back into their marriage cottage. He forgave her but the neighbours did not. They made comments whenever she passed by, not the men, but the women. My mother remained her only friend and she became known to us as Aunty Loraine.

Then there was Dr. Thomas and Mr. and Mrs. Smart. Dr. Thomas was the young parish doctor from England. People often speculated as to why a young white doctor would choose to live amongst poor blacks in a small, almost dilapidated house, which he also used as his clinic from time to time; as opposed to living with the other whites.

Some claimed he was running from the law. Some said he was half-black. Some did not trust him. Some believed the medicine he treated us with was poison. Sometimes when he made his weekly routine house visits, to those whose trust he had gained, he was greeted by nasty comments from others, for those were the times of early post slavery; wounds were still raw and bleeding.

Those were the days when distrust of 'whites' was ripe more than ever. It was hard to forget that not too long ago, that someone with his colour held the scourge—that someone like him was responsible for the many afflictions that plagued black people on the island. Those days were the days of small pox, chicken pox, measles, scabies, mumps, polio and other afflictions. Those were the days when proper health care was openly race related. However, my memory of Dr. Thomas is one of great fondness and admiration, because no matter how much some people in the village rejected him, he always came back with renewed determination. In the end he was beloved as if he had always been there amongst us.

The Smarts were the two eldest in our village. They were the village suppliers of coals and kerosene. They argued and fought all the time, over a woman that Mr. Smart was now having a clandestine relationship with. I learnt of this one day while eavesdropping on a conversation between my mother and the butcher's wife. It was speculated that the new woman had worked Obeah on Mr. Smart.

One day the heightened voices and the throwing of pots and pans stopped, and the villagers found Mrs. Smart lying in a puddle of her own blood. Mr. Smart was found a week later hanging from a Ceylon mango tree. No one dared to pick mangoes from that tree again for fear of being haunted by Mr. Smart's spirit. People said a jumbie made him do it. My mother said love was the true culprit.

The death of my eldest sister made me echo my mother's sentiments for a very long time. Years later I would learn that love is indeed a beautiful thing. However, the mistake made is thinking we are the ones meant to fight for love, when it is indeed love that fights for us. I would also grow to understand that love is a journey to be embarked upon only by the strong and whereas love can be as sweet as sugar cane itself, it could be poisonous as a venomous snake, for those who do not understand that it is not one of possession—that love transcends boundaries, time and body and thus cannot be contained—like the butterfly it must be allowed to be free in order to grow in to a thing of sheer beauty.

Susan died not too long after my father passed away. She was an ebullient soul steeped in flamboyance. She had the ability to transform the drabbest moments to giggles and frolic. We all knew of her nightly expeditions, but no one gave away her secret. We were the keepers of each other's secrets—a bond my mother vowed and sought many times to break, only to have it strengthened.

As soon as my mother turned off the kerosene lamp in the small room we shared, Susan would start preparing herself for her temporary escape. In the darkness, I would make out her slim curvy body, as she changed into her Sunday dress; the lilac coloured one with a bow at the back, the one which got her all the attention at Sunday school. After she left, I would lay there staring at the outline of the room — my brother snoring heavily on the fibre mattress on the floor, my sister deep in sleep on her side of the bed at the far end. I would toss and turn in worry until sleep seized me. I never asked Susan where she went to and who she went with but I had my suspicions.

Then one day Susan was too sick to do her daily chores or to attend school. My mother understood the signs and symptoms too well and after three or four hard slaps, Susan screamed a name. Susan was then ordered to follow my mother. I too was ordered to do the same, since we were the only ones at home. The others had left for the shop that day.

As we got nearer to the big house on the hill, I could hardly breathe from walking so fast to keep up with my mother's feisty pace.

"Mrs. McMillan!" my mother repeatedly screamed from the distance.

Even Susan's long legs could not match my mother's swift steps, so it appeared as if she was being dragged as my mother held on to her hand. It was as if our mother had gone mad. She was beyond apoplectic — barefooted, with wild dishevelled hair and wearing a dress deeply stained from condiments and ground provisions. In her eyes wavered a fire, the mad Medusa's rage. It was the first time I had ever seen that side of her and by the time we got to the big house on the hill, Mrs. McMillan was there to open the door.

The Rebellion of Mary Magdalene

Astonishment and exasperation were written all over Mrs. McMillan's pale face. At her side, almost to the back of her, stood a little boy no more than ten years old. In his tiny hand he held a wide green and white fan. He was one of those children hired and paid in food to fan away the tropical heat the whites often complained about. He was nicely attired but he wore no shoes. His straight silky black hair was neatly parted in the middle and held at the back of his head, with a piece of black string, thus accentuating his round face and large eyes. I think this was the first time I ever noticed a pair of despondent eyes, a hidden part of him almost beseeching to be rescued.

Mrs. McMillan was dressed in a long flowing white summer dress, which was popular amongst the ladies of the opulent class. She was moderately adorned in jewellery and one could say her features were strikingly beautiful, but then there was that ugly snobbish smirk which was permanently smudged on to her face, which made her look ugly and plain, a true depiction of her heart as I would later learn.

The McMillans were one of the influential and most celebrated families on our side of the island. They, unlike the rest of us had wealth and thus lived a better life. They did not live in small overcrowded houses like the majority of us. They did not eat from 'hand to mouth' like the bulk of us. Their meals did not consist of high staples—'slave food'—such as yams, dasheen, sweet potatoes and breadfruit; sometimes eaten with oil made from coconuts and if lucky, 'salt fish' was added. Chicken, beef, mutton—of that sort, were the delicacies allotted mainly for the McMillans and their kind.

They were the direct descendants of slave owners. Their massive wealth came from the brows of African slavery made legal under the British crown and thus normalized in her colonies. In the year 1807, Britain ended her slave trade. However, slavery still existed in her colonies and Africans were still being illegally transported for slave labour, through the portals of the 'black market'.

It was not until 1834 Britain went on to abolish slavery, which stated that slaves were free but still confined to the plantation, for a four-year period under a system called indentureship. This period was recorded for some as worse than slavery, for the disgruntled slave owners sought to extract every last drop of what was to be earned from slave labour. Slavery officially ended in 1838, but the mindset of many remained unchanged. Freedom meant everything to the newly freed slaves, but to those who they once called 'master' this meant nothing. A freed black person was still perceived as a slave and thus lowly in the eyes of those who once held the whip.

The McMillans had maids and three motor cars, and Mr. McMillan owned almost all the grocery stores on the island; along with three cocoa plantations, two nutmeg stations and a few acres of sugarcane. In 1714, cocoa and coffee were introduced to the island of Grenada and by the time 1843, when nutmeg was introduced, sugar production was declining. Mr. McMillan was also one of the few white sugar cane farmers left on the island. His son Paul McMillan Jr. was our Sunday school teacher and was engaged to some girl living in England — an arrangement between their parents. Everyone knew that.

The McMillans lived in a 'great house', a living monument from a haunted chapter of the island's history. Like all the other great houses on the island, it once housed slave masters and sometimes overseers within its lavish confines. Slave quarters, also known as 'slave pens', were located at the back of these great houses and they were indeed pens, for accommodations were sometimes as inhumane as they came.

These great houses would have witnessed countless tired black souls being carried in wagons from the auction house, where they had been put up for sale and bought like things. These Africans would have stood there on the auction block, dehumanized, sometimes standing naked before the eyes of many, even being groped by buyers who were given the right to inspect the human merchandise.

These black oiled bodies would have endured the harshest of conditions while traversing the middle passage across the Atlantic. They would have sat in extremely stressful positions, in the most obscene conditions; of filth, faeces and urine, diseases and immense heat with little food and water. Some would have been thrown overboard due to lack of rations on the slave ships, or as a form of punishment. Some would have flung themselves overboard rather than face a future of bondage. Either way survival was null, as sharks were known to follow the slave ships due to surety of meals. Some would have died due to ill treatment and illnesses. Some of them would have been raped and beaten to death. Those who survived the turmoil of the middle passage would have envied those whose journey had ended before the auction house.

On the plantation their conditions would have changed, not for the better but for the worse. Endless families were torn apart. Slaves were expected to work from sun up to sun down on the plantations. Food rations were given only to ensure slaves stayed alive. Many were malnourished and as if not enough, slaves were subjected to rape, murder, and torture of all kinds. The world had developed a sweet tooth and Africans were the ones that bled for it, suffered for it, but resilience was written somewhere in the story of the Africans brought to the Caribbean and other parts of the world.

My mother and Mrs. McMillan stood there staring at each other. Anger was painted in fierce colours on both their faces, more so on my mother's.

Mrs. McMillan had listened to my mother and she had listened to Susan. Her son had promised to marry Susan. He had told her he loved her. When he was called to the table he denied knowing Susan outside of Sunday school, although she had in her possession a bracelet he had given her during one of their secret rendezvous. The bracelet had come from Mrs. McMillan's very own jewellery box, she had recognized it instantly. Mrs.

McMillan then offered my mother money to carry Susan to Ole Sandra.

Ole Sandra was the name of the woman who everyone knew but never spoke about openly. She lived a very recluse life that was complementary to the role she performed.

My mother refused it, declaring vehemently, "No daughter of mine will partake in such an act!"

All the while Susan was just sitting there, quiet, lost in her own world staring at the bracelet. Despair and fear were scribbled all over her face but it was her eyes that spilled the words her heavy heart could not. She had been betrayed by the man she loved. The man who had promised to marry her. The man who had told us God said, "Stay chaste!" The man who told us, "God does not like the wicked!" The man who told us, "God is fair and one day God shall smite the wicked and uplift the righteous!" The man who told us, "Fornication is a sin and temptation and lies should be avoided!" He said Susan was delusional and that she should not accuse him of such an act.

The exchange of sword cutting words soon escalated to a scuffle between my mother and Mrs. McMillan. Mrs. McMillan had called my mother a harlot and said Susan had followed in her footsteps.

"I know your story," barked Mrs. McMillan. "You are always walking around with your nose in the air like you are the best of all those dirty niggers but you are the worst of them. I remember when you refused to work for me, because you thought yourself above the position God has given you."

My mother had turned down an offer to work for Mrs. McMillan. One Friday Mrs. McMillan made an unusual appearance at the St. George's Market Square, where my mother and I were busy weighing yams for a customer. As she stood there, blocking out the sun with her wide straw hat, making no attempt to hide her displeasure of being in the congested market, she began to explain herself, her eyes scanning the unfamiliar environment, still not making any attempt to hide the fact she thought herself superior to the rest of us. 'You are impecunious and thus unworthy' her posture and upturned nostrils screamed.

She was looking for good help. Her maid Catherine had abruptly disappeared, the day before an important event she had been planning for some time now, a grandeur gathering of the island's elites. Someone had told her that my mother was the best washerwoman and cook in our village. My mother washed and cooked two days a week for another family and sold the produce from her garden on Tuesdays and Fridays.

My mother refused the offer but not before declaring, "I will not work for someone who sees herself as better than me. As you were informed of me I was also informed of you, for if you see yourself as better than me, you can never see the virtue of my work, and if you cannot see the virtue of my hard work, then you cannot respect me and I cannot work where there is no respect."

The Rebellion of Mary Magdalene

Mrs. McMillan stormed off, trailed by an echo of laughter from the other market vendors. My mother was the only one not laughing for she meant every word she had spoken. One could describe my mother as proud and unbending in her principles—'a big stone' as she was often described by her peers.

"Madness must have befallen you if you think I will accept a nigger grandchild," Mrs. McMillan shrieked, pointing to my sister while facing my mother.

She then turned to my sister and said, "That abomination, that bastard, that devil inside of you is not from my son! You hear me! You want to marry in to a family with a good name and a white family for that matter? You take this family for those poor whites who live yonder, who like mixing and consorting with you niggers, singing and mating with your kind? A nigger grandchild in my home! Not as long as the flesh on my bones still stands—and even if death was to seize me, and I was committed to my grave, I would reach out and choke the very life from its body. Get from here! Go find your nigger for that black cursed bastard that is inside you! The blood of Jezebel runs through your veins," were her last words to Susan.

Susan just stood there wringing her hands. Her head was bowed as she retreated into herself, as Mrs. McMillan's words pierced its target and made its mark. The only time she looked up was to look at Paul McMillan, who quickly averted his eyes when he noticed Susan's eyes were on him—her eyes desperately seeking his defence. Instead he kept staring at a portrait on the wall, as if he wanted to disappear into it, as if it held some secret, as if it offered some escape from the room. The image was a family portrait of himself, Mr. McMillan and Mrs. McMillan. Mrs. McMillan was the only one smiling.

My mother shouted between clenched teeth, "Jezebel! At least we raise all our children. How many have you thrown away by Ole Sandra to keep your precious figure?"

Mrs. McMillan proceeded imprudently to slap my mother. My mother responded with a harder slap across the face of Mrs. McMillan. Then the fight started, but pampered Mrs. McMillan was no match for a woman who laboured for her daily bread. Her pale skin was quickly coloured with red and blue marks. It took two gardeners and one robust maid to remove my mother from the corner where she had Mrs. McMillan pinned down on the ground. Paul McMillan stood in the corner, traumatized by what he had just witnessed.

•••

Susan unlike my dad, was not buried in a salt fish box. My mother spent the money she had been saving for 'rainy days' to ensure my sister got a proper burial.

Susan looked so peaceful in her coffin. Her hair was neatly braided in cornrows, wearing her white dress, one hand crossed over the next on her chest. The neighbours said it was an evil spirit sent by someone who was jealous of her good looks—we knew better. Two weeks after the visit to the big house on the hill I found my sister hanging from the mango tree at the side of the house. She was sixteen and she died because of love.

After Dr. Thomas cut her down from the tree, my mother held her in her arms for what seemed as hours, singing an old chorus: *"God be with you till we meet again. By his counsels guide, uphold you. With his sheep securely fold you. God be with you till we meet again."*

The onlookers who had gathered around in disbelief and tears knew nothing about the secret that was once growing inside of her womb.

Paul McMillan later travelled to Barbados where he became a teacher. He married the girl from England and they had two beautiful boys. My sister's name was never mentioned again in our house. Her belongings were given away to people who did not know her. In order to cope, her very being was erased from our world. It was too heavy of a heartache to bear.

As a result my mother grew stricter with us. It came as no surprise when she commissioned Mr. George the carpenter, to bar the windows in our room, which allowed only thin whiffs of fresh air to pass through. Mr. George reluctantly did the work but persistently complained of the impossibility of us escaping in the event of a fire. My mother simply replied, "Death comes and goes, but not shame and heartache. They are stains that are carried."

One would think that nailing our window shut was satisfactory enough, but not so for my mother. She moved her bed outside of our bedroom door and forbade us from attending Sunday school. She even went as far as dropping the hems of our already long skirts and dresses, which earned us the nickname 'Lajabless' (*La Diablesse*) by our peers.

My mother wanted to protect her two remaining daughters from the evil rapture of love. She did what she felt was necessary to protect us. My brother was exempted from her watchful eyes.

"It is always and will always be us women, who feel the fury and wrath of love," mother said.

History is sometimes written by magicians and card players. The victor is he who can lay before his audience, the most profound mirage that the audience questions not, even when questions present themselves.

3.

History

Years and years ago, before Christopher Columbus sighted Grenada on his third voyage in the year 1498, and named her Concepción; before other Spanish sailors named her Granada, after the beautiful scenery of their homeland Andalusia; before French colonizers called Grenada La Grenade and before the British named her Grenada, she was called *Camerhogne* by the first people who inhabited the island.

The earliest people who lived on the island of Grenada were the Amerindians. The Amerindians had made the long excursion from the northern tip of South America, settling on the various islands that spanned the length of the Caribbean archipelago.

History records two groups of natives; the Caribs and the Arawaks. It is said that the Arawaks were peaceful while the Caribs were warlike and often pillaged Arawak villages. Caribbean history also records the Caribs as being cannibals. However, there is an old African proverb that declares, 'Until the lions have their own historians, tales of the hunt shall always glorify the hunter'.

In 1609 and 1638 respectively, both the British and the French attempted to settle on the untamed island of Grenada. All attempts were short-lived, as the Caribs laid steadfast resistance to their colonial ambitions. It was not until the end of the 17th century, the Europeans, specifically the French, finally succeeded to establish their presence on the island of Grenada. Nevertheless, hostility continued between the Caribs and the French, due to their brazenness—the irrational and sinister ambitions of the invaders.

The final battle and the one which dealt a harsh blow to the existence of the Caribs, was the battle that occurred at the northern tip of the island. It is said, that the Caribs having accepted their defeat at the hands of the French soldiers, simply jumped off a precipice; and again as the old African proverb goes, 'Until the lions have their own historians, tales of the hunt shall always glorify the hunter'. This place of alleged 'mass suicide', was thereafter referred to as '*Le Morne de Sauteurs*' in the tongue of the conquerors. It later became known as 'Leapers Hill'.

The island then saw a turnover of power from French to British rule under the Treaty of Paris. The treaty ended a seven year war between the two colonial powers, as they continued their savage scramble for the tiny islands of the Lesser Antilles.

Thereafter, large influxes of Africans were recorded. Thousands were brought to Grenada and other Caribbean islands under British rule. Britain just like the French and the Dutch and the Portuguese and the Spanish were responsible for the removal of millions of Africans from their homeland. The great beloved colonial powers, 'upholders of all things civil', had succeeded in disrupting the very civilization of a whole continent for their own evil and selfish financial gains, and the world turned a blind eye as demands for sugar, tobacco, corn, cotton, coffee, spices, indigo and many other cash crops were met.

The end of African slavery did not bring about any profound turning of the tides, however many changes occurred. The commencement of the indentureship period in the late 18th century resulted in the immigration of Portuguese from Madeira, East Indians from India and other immigrants from Sierra Leone and Malta. New people from diverse lands, added more levels to the hierarchy of the Caribbean. However, the lowly position allotted for those of African origin remained the same.

•••

This was the summary of what our teacher told us during history lessons. I loved history lessons. I loved the fact that the Caribs stood up against tyranny and imperialism, even to their deaths.

I used to daydream about standing with the Caribs— my face and body fiercely attired with tribal paintings, a spear in my hand—the golden rays of the sun bouncing off the tip of the carved stone at the end, the bow and arrow waiting on my back, a crescent shaped pendant around my neck. I would have chosen the path of the Carib warrior. I thought it a brave and honourable thing to fight and die for a good cause.

I also loved the story of Julien Fedon. I loved how he rose up to stand against the injustices of the British in 1795. I used to sit hours upon hours, imagining myself walking side by side with Mr. Fedon, hiding in trees, lying in wait in the mountain mist for the enemies of freedom—aiding in the plot to uproot British tyrannical rule. If I were there, the British would have never defeated us. I would have ensured that we won. I would have crushed Britain and any other colonial power, be it French, Dutch or Spanish, I often thought.

I could not see myself working as a slave. 'Yes massa' was a hideous idea for me to accept. At that age I could not fathom enduring slavery. Later on in my life I found out that the ability of the African people to endure slavery for so long, is indicative of their strength, immense power, and obviously immense patience and resilience.

One day during History lesson, Miss Burris asked us if we had any questions. I raised my hand and I could tell she was displeased to see my hand up. She always seemed irritated by the questions I asked. After my hand had grown tired and all the students had asked their questions, she finally gestured in my direction. I guess she was hoping the bell for the lunch period would sound, but it did not.

I then questioned, "Miss Burris, how could Columbus have discovered an island that already had Caribs and Arawaks living on it? Is it not true that the Caribs and the Arawaks discovered Grenada because they were the first ones here; and if a people were to invade Grenada today, would you not fight to keep your home? I think the Europeans made up stories about the Caribs being aggressive war-like cannibals, because they wanted to justify their wicked actions."

I was in standard 5 and about to sit the Entrance Exam when Miss Burris responded in a reproachful voice, "Why are you like that? Teachers tell you one thing and you want to think and say the other. Say what I taught you, not what you think up in that rude head of yours and I tell you already, that girls like you who like to ask questions and don't know their place never make it far eh! Girls like you end up pregnant with no husband! You too fresh! Exams coming up, write what I tell you!"

I wrote what she taught us in class on the exam paper, but in my head the sainted stories of Columbus, the villainizing of the Caribs never sat right with me.

I also despised Bartholomew de las Casas. Miss Burris had told us he was sympathetic to the evils done to the Amerindians—the rape, the abuse, the torture, the enslavement by the Europeans, but why was he not sympathetic to the plight of the Africans? I thought him and Christopher Columbus to be bad men, but I knew better than to reveal my thoughts aloud, so most times I kept them safe in my head while in Miss Burris's class.

On that day when Miss Burris had lectured me on becoming pregnant I had snapped back, "If women don't get pregnant, there will be no one here on earth, but I am not going to get pregnant because one day I will lead a revolution just like Mr. Julien Fedon and I will win."

I said it with conviction but I was not convinced. I was a little school girl, how and when would I start and win a revolution? Nevertheless, the entire class erupted into unrestrained laughter, which seemed to make Miss Burris even more irate from the series of 'bad eyes' she flashed me.

I was sent to the principal's office to receive five strokes. My punishment was administered with a thick leather belt that was previously soaked in stale urine for children like myself. My red-brown swollen skin felt as if it was on fire after the flogging and I reeked of a repugnant odour. I was mortified. However, I managed to smile within, for I had stood up to Miss Burris. I felt like I was standing up for my rights, just as Mr. Fedon had done, just as the Caribs had done against the French.

In those days regular beatings at home and school were seen as good Grenadian parenting. 'Licks' was the best way to instill discipline—'spare not the rod and spoil the child', but from my own experience beatings only made me bitter and resentful of authoritative figures.

I never understood the rationale behind the use of leather belts—especially the buckle; bull pistle, tamarind whips, machine cords, kneeling on a grater while holding two heavy stones above the head. I was baffled that the children of slaves employed the same inhumane methods once used on their fore-parents. I found it appalling that parents would equate this kind of abuse to love. How could they not see the physical, emotional, mental and spiritual trauma that kind of 'love' brought forth? Their arguments always being that this method worked for them. How could they not see!

My mother was not pleased with my behaviour. Miss Burris had added more to what I had said in class that day, and my mother proportionally added another flogging to the previous one I had received in school. I hated Miss Burris for a long time afterwards. I hated her as much as I hated Christopher Columbus. I hated her as much as I hated the Europeans for oppressing the Amerindians and the Africans.

Consequently, I made it my duty to disrupt her classes with questions I knew she hated. In time I would learn that Miss Burris, like every person I had crossed paths with, was merely playing her role in a greater plan—a brick, to build a house of compassion, wisdom and love.

One of God's creations roared and from her fiery womb she birthed islands. Hence our passion! Hence our fire! Hence our everlasting beauty and resilience!

4.

The Isle of Spice

I understand why people fought for control over this place. As a child I saw the island as magically enchanting and that feeling enhanced as I grew older. The island was replete with lush green vegetation, breathtaking mountains adorned with the white crowns of silk cottons and the flaming torches of flamboyant trees, fruits trees of all sorts—juicy mangoes, so juicy that the nectar ran down your hand when you bit into one, mouth-watering red and yellow plums, tasty soursops disguised in prickly skins, sapodillas and sugar apples as sweet as honey, big ripe guavas that enticed you with their gentle aroma and exotic taste; mammy apples and golden apples ready to eat on the spot or to make sweet jams, and the list of other delicious tropical fruits were endless.

Then there were the rivers, cascading waterfalls, freshwater lakes, bays and emerald inlets, gushing freshwater springs, mangroves, sulphur springs ideal for a good scrub; and the island's wildlife echoing in the forests; mona monkeys and beautiful birds mimicking the colours of the rainbow, green iguanas and others that remained too shy or hidden. Grenada was magical in my eyes. Grenada was enchanting to all whose eyes beheld her.

My mother's garden was located in a rather mountainous part of the island called Morne Jaloux, overlooking the capital town of St. George's. This roller coaster mountain range of high ridges and lush valleys was named by the French colonizers and it translates to 'jealous mountains', in the language of our most recent colonizers.

Every Saturday morning my family and I made our way past Fort Frederick. A living relic forged from the colonial history of Grenada, and from there one could see another preserved monument in the distance, Fort George. These two enormous stone fortresses were built to keep out invaders; powerful black cannons pointing out to the open sea, reminding passers-by of what they once were—a force not to be reckoned with, bringers of death, the ones who had sunk many naval ships.

I remember often wondering about the people who laboured to build those forts. What were they like? What were their names? Of course, history remembers only the inhabitants of the house, most rarely the builders. It must have taken great effort to build what once were and still are, structures of such magnificence. In the belly of these forts lay tunnels soldiers had once used to transport and store supplies and as a place to cower when the cannons blasted.

If those tunnels could speak, I am sure they would tell tales of mutinous plots, of desperate hearts longing to return home, regrets, the whispers of dying men as they exerted their last breaths, calling maybe to some loved one in a faraway land—professing their eternal love and calling to God, asking him to keep their souls safe, begging for forgiveness for their earthly trespasses—many young, some old.

So many men had fought and died for colonial powers that grew richer by the acquisition of lands that was not rightfully theirs to begin with; men of poor backgrounds made to fight each other, duped into thinking they were fighting for a greater cause—but instead what they were really fighting for was the appeasement of the insatiable greed of rich men, who created wars and cared nothing about the desolation that came with it. Numerous men had fallen on this beautiful island called Grenada, but no matter how ugly the war, the temptress Grenada with all her allure and promises kept her enchanting beauty and buoyancy.

The scenery that lay before Fort Frederick often drew me into its own world; the natural harbour, the sparkling blue sea, the rooftops of small huts that spanned out in different directions along the uneven contours and foothills of the fort. Then there was Her Majesty's Prison, which was built in 1860 by the French as a military hospital and then converted in 1880 to a prison. Years later, I would pay a visit to an inmate there. I would shed tears when I noticed how meagre and miserable looking he had become—those unforgiven walls had sucked him to a skeletal ghostly state. He would tell me that he was being singled out by a guard for regular beatings and inhumane labour. I would hold his hands and reassure him, "I will avenge you."

Some years later fate would whisper in my ear, "I come to those who beckon to me. I weigh their cries justly and when the scale is unbalanced, I am compelled to bring it back to its natural order."

...

My mother had acquired the fertile piece of land in compensation for her services, to an elderly woman whom she had cared for when she first came to the island. I was not yet conceived when my mother worked for her, but her name is forever knitted in my mind because my mother spoke highly of her and very often too.

She often said, "Mrs. Henry was as hard as a dry coconut but kind and loving." A beautiful smile would then wash over her face as she recounted stories of Mrs. Henry to us.

Mrs. Henry's father had owned many plantations in Jamaica, all of which she inherited when he passed away since she was an only child. However, a young Mrs. Henry was far from being a proper lady. She wore trousers and swore like an English sailor and had absolutely no table manners as the other ladies of her time. Her mother had died whilst giving birth to her and so she was raised as the son her father always wanted. It was for those 'unladylike' qualities she was never proposed to or pursued like the other women. In those times, the expectations for ladylike decorum was ingrained in every aspect of society. Mrs. Henry was the embodiment of unladylike.

At the tender age of twenty while overseeing one of her plantations from the tall of her favourite white horse, with sweat pouring from every part of her body, a young handsome man stumbled onto the grounds asking for directions. He was the most handsome man she had ever seen and as luck would have it, they were very compatible in thinking, or so she thought. They married the following year and moved to Grenada, away from the watchful eyes of her uncle, whom she had hired to help her with the affairs of the plantations.

Her uncle was against the union of the new couple and accused the young teacher of being suspiciously cunning and desperately ambitious. Over the years she bore him three children. Some nights he made it home, most nights he did not. On the nights he did manage to come home to her she was grateful, because she was deeply in love with him. She was never one to compromise before, but blind foolish love had conspired to weaken her.

The old woman died in her room with only my mother at her bedside. Her husband had left her for a younger woman, a mutual friend whom Mrs. Henry had taken in under her roof due to a scandal of 'ruined reputation' in England.

The Rebellion of Mary Magdalene

Anne was her name. She was the cousin of Mrs. Henry's uncle by marriage. At some point in her life Mrs. Henry considered Anne James to be a dear friend and confidant. They both knew what it felt like to be ostracised. On many days they swapped stories in which Mrs. Henry lamented about the emotional, verbal, physical and financial abuse she suffered at the hands of her 'prim and proper' fiend of a husband. In turn Anne James confided in Mrs. Henry, about the romantic affair with the man she had fallen in love with, a married man. They were both broken women—but only one knew the meaning of honour.

As for Mrs. Henry's three children, they were living in England and only wrote to her when they needed money. The letters always started with greetings of love followed by its real intent, an overbearing entitlement to her wealth. She had made the error of leaving her children's upbringing to her husband and so her three sons were carbon copies of their father.

At her funeral her husband and children arrived rather pompously. They were eager to make their claim on the wealth Mrs. Henry had left behind, but as the lawyer read the will the old woman had her final revenge.

My mother was to be given a vast piece of land and some money along with some books, and to her children, handwritten scripture verses that would torment even the devil if he had a conscience. As for her husband, he inherited a piece of rope, a piece of white stale bread— overrun with green moss, and a glass of water; and to her once best friend, she left a note which read: '*My sleep has begun and so will your torment*'. Her six estates, monies, jewelleries and lands were to be given to the church as atonement for her sins.

My mother said that the old woman was the closest thing she had to a mother on the island. I believe it was from her my mother inherited her strength or maybe it was life itself and the many lessons it had taught her. Either way, my mother and Mrs. Henry were indeed strong women.

Our genesis is of the soil, our middle is of the soil and in the end, we shall be returned to the soil.

5.

Gardening

On some mornings, sometimes at the same time we were leaving for school, my mother would set off to her garden. One could have easily mistaken her for an old woman, in her raggedy brown or black dress that dropped midway over her smooth, velvet-like brown calves. On her head she wore a hat, neatly weaved from coconut leaves—weaved by her own hands.

The wide brim of the hat hid an exquisite face, birthed from the ancestry of white Portuguese, Kalinago, Indian and African features. Her matted long black hair was always kept in a neat bun at the back of her head, or neatly covered with head wraps that mimicked the rainbow. Her beautiful almond shaped brown eyes, white pearly teeth, flared nostrils and thick even lips complimented her slender face—an exotic beauty she was indeed. She was neither tall nor short. She was neither quiet nor talkative and like the monarch butterfly, many knew it was better to stay afar.

The Rebellion of Mary Magdalene

Saturday was the day we all went to the garden. In the dark eerie hours of the morning, guided by the kerosene lamp and candles, we would all work in unison to complete the tasks of preparing our food for the trip to Morne Jaloux. It was my brother's job to fetch the coal pot and to get the fire started. I remember his childish giggles from seeing his own hands blackened from the chalky coals. I remember him sometimes dabbing some on the side of his cheeks and dancing wildly, until our mother came out from wherever she was, hands on her wide hips and fire in her eyes. We would all laugh and return to our chores.

My sister and I were charged with preparing the breadfruit, yams, coconut milk and dumplings. Our hands would move skillfully back and forth, to remove the skin from the staples with the black handle knife; our fingers mixing together white flour and corn flour, then kneading the mixture to a firm rock. I recall our innocent laughter from playing with our dancing shadows, as we took turns grating the creamy coconuts. We would giggle uncontrollably when our brother joined in to make figure shadows also and again my mother would appear and warn us to make haste as she did not want the morning sun to catch us. Our mother would busy herself tidying the house. Her famous saying was, "You may not be the queen of England, but your house can still be as clean as the queen's palace."

In the end, we would all gather around the coal pot, as it cooked the contents of the wide black-belly pot that my mother had neatly packed with the ingredients we had prepared. The sweet aroma of the rich coconut milk simmering with grated saffron, flooded our nostrils; whiffs of sweet peppers and other local seasonings and the distinct smell of the salt fish, together bubbling away, made making our bellies rumble and our salivary juices flow.

As we waited patiently, my mother would recite to us stories of Bre'r Anansi and all his tricks, and we would fill ourselves with laughter to our hearts' delight, forgetting the emptiness of our stomachs. However, before the break of dawn we would be out of the house—with 'good food' and black sage tea in our bellies, we would start the journey to our mother's garden.

Along the way we often met other farmers heading to tend their own plots of land. The area my mother owned was expansive, mostly flat with gentle slopes. On one part of it, she planted yams, dasheen, sweet potatoes, peppers and many other short crops. On another plot, she cultivated sugarcane which was sold to the sugar factory. When the sugarcane was ready, all the other farmers in the area would pitch in to assist her. It was customary for farmers to help each other during land preparation and harvest time.

My mother was a hard worker. Preservation of one's beauty by avoiding hard labour and the sun was far from her thoughts—yet still, she was regarded as the most beautiful woman in our village. My sister Susan was born with the same physical likeness as my mother. Their looks were unmatched and often talked about; like the time my mother sent me to the shop to purchase a piece of salt fish and I had to stand there, for almost ten minutes listening to Mr. Rolo and a customer, blabbering about how beautiful and appealing my mother was.

I stood there, impatiently listening until I got tired and then I loudly exclaimed, "Mr. Rolo, my mother say you have a woman in your house and you must stop calling her out when she passing about she business. She say she doh want no man who have woman already. She doh want any man like you! Mr. Rolo my mother don't want you."

I was angry. The words flew out of my mouth as an angry finch. I was astonished at myself. The two men were even more astounded. Mr. Rolo and the customer both looked at me at the same time, their mouths opened at what I had just said. In those days, a child of my age dared not say such things to an adult. In those days, adults were kings and queens, and we were just tiny servants susceptible to punishment whenever they saw it befitting.

I then explained swiftly, "My mother say she wants the salt fish now to cook for us, and she say if I take long she go blaze my backside, so give me the salt fish and let me go home."

My mother did say the second part. The first part was a total fabrication, but I assumed that was what she would say in response to Mr. Rolo talking so vulgarly about the shape of her behind.

As a child I particularly disliked Mr. Rolo, and looking back I can see how our fear of a person, could sometimes stir up a false sense of hatred and scorn. It was said that Mr. Rolo was a '*Loupgarou*'. I remember one day hearing my mother's friend recall a story of being up late one full moon night and witnessing Mr. Rolo's transformation. She claimed she saw him shed his skin and turned into a ball of flaming red fire. She swore she witnessed him going from house to house in his changed form.

I remember my mother buying extra salt, from the man who often brought her salt from the salt pond located on the far south-western part of the island. On the inside of the doors and windows of our house, she would scatter generous portions, mumbling that it was to keep Mr. Rolo from entering our home and strange enough the red marks that often appeared in the most intimate places—on her legs, thighs and arms stopped appearing. However, we heard other complaints elsewhere, of women waking up to find themselves shaved in the most private of places. It was even said that some men woke up to find shaved hair on their faces, pasted on to form a moustache. Nevertheless, people still flocked to Mr. Rolo's small flourishing business due to his fair prices, secretly praying he would not enter into their homes at night.

I was ten years old when Mr. Rolo told me, "You fresh up and rude too much. You ent go make it far in this world. You ent go make it far in this world at all."

That day I quietly made a vow to myself, to show him that I was no little girl to be tampered with, and that I would grow up and become someone of importance, someone who would challenge men like him, who saw women as mere flesh on the butcher's table.

He stopped harassing my mother after that, but he took his revenge by making me wait longer each time my mother sent me to the shop. What did I care! I had succeeded in putting Mr. Rolo's tongue where it belonged, back in his mouth, safe in his head. I had succeeding in standing up to the most reputed *loupgarou* in our village.

...

My sister Paulette hated gardening. Paul and I were always excited about going to the garden. Paul and Paulette were twins. So in that order we were born, Paul and Paulette, then me. Susan was the first. At the end of the day we would load up big brown crocus bags on our heads and make our way down to a little house, close to the St. George's Market Square. There my mother had a friend who sold her produce on the days she was preoccupied with other responsibilities. In return she paid her friend a certain percentage of the produce.

As a reward for our good behaviour and hard labour, my mother would reward us with one penny each to purchase a snowball—shaved ice smothered in a sweet thick syrup. It was truly a treat in the hot biting Grenadian sun and on the days when we were we extremely well behaved and my mother had enough money to spare, she would buy us Mr. Slinger's rich and creamy ice-cream as an additional treat. Bestlait ice-cream was the most sought after ice-cream in those times—vanilla, chocolate, strawberry and local flavours would lure customers from far and wide. It was the taste to die for, a taste from the heavens. *C'était un goût à mourir de plaisir, tout droit tombé du ciel.*

At the end of the day, giddy with joy, we would make our way to where the large board buses waited eagerly in the market square to be filled with passengers—buses with names such as 'Creole Pride', 'Creole', 'Live and let live', 'Hey Leroy', 'Joint Effort', 'Western Hope', 'B.G Pride', 'Sweet Roses', elegantly painted on them. When filled to capacity, these big buses with opened spaces for windows and wooden frames painted in varying colours, would begin their slow earthworm like pace to their various destinations.

As we moved off, the cacophony of battering and bickering over market prices and the incessant calls of vendors, "Come get your oranges, nice and sweet! Any breadfruit for you today? Miss, nice paw-paw, nice tannia, sweet potatoes!" would fade out, and the heavy hum of the engine would preside boldly.

People see what they believe, or is it that belief reveals certain things?

6.

Obeah

It was my first time meeting her.

"Mary, come here darling," my aunt commanded lovingly.

She was six years younger than my mother but one could never tell. They were identical in personality as well as looks. However, where my mother remained silent on certain issues, my aunt was extremely vocal. On numerous occasions she would go on and on about how women should strive to get into politics. She would say, "Only women go look out for women."

I took a liking to her instantly. She said she had grown weary of working at Mr. Ching's shop, so she said goodbye to her friends and left Trinidad. Mr. Ching had offered to raise her pay, but her mind was already made up. Her destination was Grenada to be reunited with her sister.

On the same day my aunt showed up on our doorsteps, I found a purse with some money on my way home from the butcher. This time I did not share my findings with my siblings, as it was customary amongst us to always divide whatever we had. This time I kept it for myself, and for Karl.

Karl was the village reject who went around doing the dirty work no one wanted to do themselves. We became friends on the day my mother hired him to dig us a new pit latrine. He had confessed that my mother was the kindest person he had ever met, for instead of paying him in leftover food like most people did, she paid him 'fair and square', the price she would pay anyone to do such a job, and still rewarded him with a big plate of hot food and some clothing.

I took the money to the shop and ordered the items my mother usually bought—as to not raise suspicion, for I knew if my mother found out she would say return the money to the place where I found it. In those days, people were convinced that money lying idly around was a way people sold other people to the devil, especially young children.

One time my mother told us about a man, who had a five dollar note that always returned to him after he spent it. According to my mother, the man had sold his only son to the devil in return for that favour. However, one day the St. George's Market Square was at a standstill, as fear, shock and sheer panic took hold of everyone. The very said green five dollar note was being pulled left and right in mid-air by unseen forces. She said that the man who had sold his son was caught in a battle for the five dollar bill, with a well know 'Obeah man', who was also a vendor and was very determined to be paid for his produce. She ended the story there and I guess my mother was not a very convincing storyteller, for the fear of being sold to the devil seemed too preposterous to take seriously.

Another memory from my earlier childhood that sticks out as a sore thumb, was the day I was taken to Ole Mary by the river. The acute illness that had befallen me had done so very suddenly. I was playing outside one minute and then I was bed-ridden the next minute. First I experienced a burning fever that turned my bed into a lake as sweat poured from my pores. I felt like the sun was sitting right next to me, whispering spells into my ear; then the continuous vomiting followed, so much so, I remained hoarse as my throat became too blistered to form any intelligible sounds. Then came the boils on my skin, oozing yellow-green pus which left a stench so pungent, it made my own stomach hurl.

Dr. Thomas was called in and his medication did not bring much relief nor any promise of recovery whatsoever. I was in bed for two weeks when the decision was made. I was between sleep, painful discomfort and fear when I overheard the conversation between my mother and my aunt.

"I am not taking her to no Obeah woman," I heard my mother say.

"Well we have to and you know who did this and if we don't do anything she will die and then what?" asked my aunt. "Can you live with that?" she continued, "Dr.

Thomas's medicine cannot fix this. If anything, his medication has made her worse. This is not any infection from his big book. He is not one of us; he cannot cure this. This is Obeah! I love her just as you do," my aunt went on to say.

"But why would she want to hurt her? She is an innocent child," my mother finally surrendered.

I remember being lifted and placed in Mr. Paloma's donkey cart—the smell of sweat and manure clung tightly to the stained board floor. I remember being wrapped in a thick grey wool blanket to keep the chilly night air out, as my teeth clattered violently together and my whole body quivered in uncontrolled spasms. I remember seeing my mother's worried and unsettled face in the sparse light. My aunt's face looked just the same. I remember the bumpy ride as we took the path to the river. I remember being carefully taken out from Mr. Paloma's cart and being put on his back, that had grown strong from farming. My mother walked behind him to lend support, to prevent my head from jolting backwards, for I was too weak to even keep my own body steady as he carefully crossed over and in between river stones.

I remember my aunt walking alongside him with a lamp like the one my mother held in her hand, so that he could see his way through the darkness. I remember when Mr. Paloma took a fall. I remember hearing my mother and my aunt's voice just before I slipped into an unconscious state. I remember their frantic voices—the raw panic.

I heard Mr. Paloma's deep voice when he shrieked distressfully, "She going! God help us!"

The next thing I remember was being in a small strange room. I remember seeing the face of Ole Mary. She smiled when she saw me looking at her and remarked, "They send evil spirit for you. You made somebody angry girl."

I was too weak to reply, but I watched as she started shouting and swaying her body in short, slow, rhythmic movements and speaking in a language unknown to my ears at that time. She suddenly stopped and from the shelf she removed a huge book —a book ten times thicker than the slate I wrote on at school—and she started reading in the same unknown language. She then gave me a sweet brown liquid in a small calabash to drink. My head bobbed up and down to sip the content of the bowl as Ole Mary gently held me upright at her side, as my entire body was simply too weak to carry out the task on its own. Afterwards she rubbed my body with a strange smelling concoction, while reciting in the language that was foreign to my ear.

Two days later I was back in the road playing cricket and marbles. My mother never spoke of that night. My aunt never spoke of that night. That night I felt something hot and heavy leave my body. Maybe it was the sickness, but something left. I also never spoke of it but I often wondered about the payment Ole Mary had received for saving me.

The Rebellion of Mary Magdalene

That night when the heaviness left my body, Ole Mary had pointed her finger at a particular spot in the room, as if talking to someone and she commanded, "Leave this place. You have no place here! Go back to the evil soul that sent you for this poor child!" A gale of wind or what seemed like it, suddenly flew out the door and then there was a spine-chilling silence that flooded the dimly lit room.

The questions of today will become the paragraphs of tomorrow.

7.

Fresh Start

I felt different on the first day I started secondary school. Maybe it was due to the fact all my school things were new as opposed to the customary 'hand-me-downs' from my older sister. Maybe I felt different due to the fact I was exempted from doing the morning chores that day—no washing of breakfast wares, no 'sweeping up' of the flowers that had fallen from the yellow poui tree, which stood at the front of our house, no milking of the cow and the five goats that gave us fresh milk.

On that morning my mother served us cocoa tea and buttered coconut bakes, baked in the outside drum oven—a special breakfast that was usually reserved for Friday and Sunday mornings.

I was beyond elated. I had dreamt of attending secondary school for what seemed like an eternity. In reaction to my obvious excitement my brother Paul remarked, "Don't feel too special. Prison is prison."

Paul was a student at what is today called the Grenada Boys Secondary School. In our time the school was called the St. George's Grammar School. Its doors were opened on February 2, 1885 and first started off with only ten boys belonging to the rising middle class and upper class of the island. As time progressed, the opportunity and privilege to attend a secondary school was extended to the lower class on the island, which mainly consisted of the descendants of African slaves.

Paul did not share my enthusiasm for school and made no attempt to hide it. He would often say, "I don't want to be no lawyer and doctor. I want to be the man who feeds them. People cannot eat books and money. I want to be the man who always has the food."

Hence, on many mornings, it was either his shoes that went missing or his pants. Either way he always found them whenever my mother appeared with the thick brown strap and that singular look on her face.

On our way to school that first morning, sitting in the back of Mr. Leroy's board bus, we stopped and a girl dressed in the same uniform that I was wearing, mounted. She smiled as she took the empty seat in front of me and I returned the same smile effortlessly, for there was something familiar and enchanting about her — as if I knew her from somewhere or we had met before. Everyone but Paul and his friend with the big ears and wide gap in his front teeth kept quiet throughout the journey. 'River mouth' was Paul's nickname.

Along the way, I could not help but admire the tropical scenery as the heavy bus chugged on. There were thick groves of green trees everywhere along the winds and bends of the thin road; students in different uniforms from the St. George's Government School, Wesley Hall, St. George's Anglican School and other schools lined the poorly paved route to be picked up by a bus. On their feet some wore slippers, others wore 'chiney shoes' and 'dog muzzles', while some simply wore none at all, a total contrast to their well attired upper bodies. Some people were simply walking, while others were carrying loads of varying sorts—some were carrying large bowls filled with homemade sweets; some were carrying green bananas on their heads; some were carrying pails of fresh cow's milk with soursop branches as a covering to alleviate spillage. I suspected they were making their way to the Carenage to sell the milk to Mr. Slinger, so he could make his tasty ice cream. Motor vehicles were sparse in those days and vehicles had to perform a range of manoeuvres to get pass each other on the narrow roads.

I had noticed all this on many occasions but that particular day was special. I was agog to witness my new school and I was determined to not let anything spoil the day. The previous night I had a terrible dream. I dreamt I was being chased by the white woman again. This time no Ole Mary came to save me. It was my mother who woke me when she heard me screaming. When I recounted the dream to her she reassured, "She cannot harm you. God is in charge." She gave no further explanation and I left it as that.

...

Our school was one of the first secondary schools to be established on the island. It was everything I had envisioned, since before the results from the Entrance Exam were announced in the assembly hall by the principal of my former school. Girls were everywhere. Some I knew or had seen before. Some I was seeing for the very first time. The spacious grounds, the neatly painted concrete buildings, were properly kept and the older students were directing the new students to the assembly hall. I was home, finally.

After the Monday morning assembly, we all headed to our different classrooms. Our classroom was comfortable and ample in space. Chairs and tables were neatly lined up in rows and on the walls hung inspirational quotes from eminent persons. Our form mistress then directed each one of us to our seat. Surprisingly, sitting next to me was the same girl from the bus. She smiled in my direction again and her warm countenance persuaded me to respond with an amicable beam of my own.

After we had all settled into our seats, we were asked to stand, row by row, one at a time, and to repeat our names and where we lived and our hobbies and future aspirations. I learnt that the girl's name was Liz Bishop. Her hobby was reading. We lived in the same area but strangely I had never seen her before. She wanted to be a lawyer like her father. I instantly fell in love with the articulated manner in which she pronounced her words, not shaky and unsure like the other girls, but with a breath of ebullience. When it was my turn, I followed her example in pronouncing my name, mimicking her confidence.

When I was finished and the next girl stood up to say her own part, I found myself wondering why Liz took the board bus to school with us when her father was a lawyer. Board buses packed tightly with children and adults — like slave ships, like sardines in a tin, were for the poor kind, my kind. I then started daydreaming. I saw myself getting out of a motor car. I then imagined my father was in the driver's seat. I then imagined him smiling at me as I waved goodbye to him, as I had seen a girl wave to her father after he dropped her off that morning, but of course all that was imagination, for 'that man' was dead and 'that man' never owned a motor car. 'That man' was a 'that man'.

As I listened to the other girls talk about their families, I felt a sudden surge of rage mixed with sadness and pity. Why couldn't God have given me a lawyer for a father like Liz? I thought. Why couldn't God have given me a doctor for a father, as Patricia's father? Patricia was the name of the girl seated behind me. Why couldn't God have given me a dentist for a father, as Elizabeth's father? Elizabeth was the name of the girl sitting adjacent to Liz. She was fair in complexion with dull red freckles scattered on the gentle mounds of her face. Her flaming red hair was neatly braided into two large plaits that fell all the way down to her shoulders. At least my hair is longer than hers, I thought. At least my hair is curlier than hers, I thought. At least I don't have spots on my face, I thought.

At break time, the girls separated into groups. There were thirty one girls in my classroom. The fair-skinned ones gathered in a well protected group. The taller girls huddled together in another corner. The shorter girls grouped up in another. The girls whose fathers had dropped them off in motor cars formed another batch and then there was us—Ruth, Liz and me.

My mother once told me that I had gotten my long curly hair from the grandmother I never met. I had 'good hair' as she called it. At least I have long hair, I reminded myself that morning. It could have been worse, I told myself. I could have been like Ruth. Ruth's hair was the complete opposite of mine and most of the other girls. Her hair was short and thick and she was a lot darker than the rest of us.

At least I have beautiful hair, I remarked silently. It could have been worse, I told myself. I could have been Ruth.

At the end of the school day, our form mistress Miss John came again, but this time to make us recite our prayers. Miss John was neither short nor tall. She had a beautiful oval face with high cheekbones and a pronounced forehead, that stood out from her hair being pulled in a tight bun at the back of her head. In the middle of her left cheek was a small deep sink, a single dimple. While most people had to smile for their dimple to be revealed, Miss John's dimple appeared effortlessly.

The Rebellion of Mary Magdalene

We often gossiped about the strangeness of her having one dimple, for it was believed that one dimple was a result of being kissed by the devil. Miss John was one of those people who spoke well and believed firmly in discipline. Every day after saying our prayers, she would remind us about the proper conduct expected for young ladies—"No chewing of gum on the road, no loud noise on the road, no talking to boys, no eating mangoes while walking home, no eating at all, only silence. Little girls are seen and not heard," she would remind us convincingly, and each time I found myself wondering if Paul was being told these things at his school. If they did, the boys never took any heed, because they were always eating and speaking from the highest pitch of their voices, and even coquetting shamelessly with every girl that passed by.

It was only us girls who bowed our heads in meek silence I noticed. We were the ones who took heed. If one of us broke the rule, she had to endure the walk of shame amongst her peers and teachers, and worst her own parents. We had enough fear to keep us in line. We were 'good girls' and 'good girls were seen and not heard'. 'Good girls' obeyed the rules. I was a 'good girl' and so were Liz and Ruth. We were 'good girls'.

•••

When I placed first in form 2 in our annual class promotional exams, my mother bought me a beautiful stylish red dress. Maybe it was symbolic, for I saw my first period earlier that year. I was in school when it happened. I recall feeling an irrepressible pain in my lower abdomen and asking permission to visit the washroom during English class. The teacher looked at me and scolded, "learn to hold it! You are not at primary school anymore!" So I sat there quietly in discomfort, twisting and turning in my mind and pretended to learn. As soon as the break bell sounded, I bolted for the washroom and to my horror a large blood stain had already soiled my underwear. I was terrified.

In my ignorance I imagined this was a sure sign of cancer, for my mind suddenly recalled a conversation between my mother and my aunt, about a woman who had died from cancer that affected that part of the body. For a good long time I stood there in pain, just staring at the red discolouration of my flour bag underclothing. When I told the English teacher what happened, she sent me home early with a note addressed to my mother. Upon reading the note my mother gave me a piece of diaper cloth to place between my legs and for the pain in my stomach, I was treated with a bitter remedy drawn from guava buds and lemongrass steeped in hot water. It wasn't until later I learnt the facts from Liz, who seemed to be well informed on what a menstrual cycle was. When I told her she smiled and said, "Welcome to the birth of beautiful things."

My mother's reaction was quite the opposite. A great sadness grew on her face as she read the note I had given to her. Her only words were, "Make sure you stay away from boys."

The Rebellion of Mary Magdalene

The teacher who wrote the note was Miss Lee. I remember her telling me, "Just make sure you keep those legs of yours closed. Little girls these days are like female dogs in heat. All the hard work we put in here and all they can think about is fornication and boys. Where I am from we call girls like that *'salope'*. Do you want to be known as a *'salope'*?" she asked me coldly.

I instinctively nodded as I suspected it was the response she wanted. She was from the island of Martinique. I did not know the meaning of the word *'salope'* at the time but I remember hearing my mother use it to describe a woman she despised. My mother and my aunt often spoke in patois to each other, when discussing topics far too advanced for our ears—'big people business' as it was called. Liz later told me the meaning of the word and I wondered if there was such a word reserved for men and if men were also referred to as *'salope'*, after all it seemed fair.

...

In the final exam for our promotion to form 2, Liz placed first in the class. I placed second. When the teacher read out the grades I was angry and disappointed and I made no attempt to hide it. On our way home Liz tried to hold my hand as we always did, but I flung her hand away distastefully and strutted ahead. I even stopped talking to her for a week until she brought me a gift— mango stew from her home. She then hugged me and said she missed me and that she loved me. I was astonished because no one had ever told me they loved me before, not even my mother or my siblings. In response, I managed to mumble, "Ok,we are still friends."

Looking back I can say Liz was more than a good friend. So much so, that when I placed first in form 2 in the end of term promotional exam, Liz appeared more excited and happier than I was. Liz placed second. The following day she brought me a big bottle of guava jam. Ruth on the other hand, placed fourth in form 1 and last in form 2. However she was promoted on terms of good behaviour. Nevertheless, the three of us were inseparable. At school we would sit together during the recesses allotted for morning break and lunch. On our way home from school we would hold hands and speak in the mildest of tones, fearful we would break the 'little girls are seen and not heard' honour code. We were 'good girls'.

...

A phenomenon that occurred when I started form 2 was the return of an abandoned tradition—of attending church and Sunday school. One Sunday morning my mother simply got up and 'out of the blues' ordered us to church. We had not done so in years since the death of Susan.

When we got to the church, we were inspected by some older women, whose sole purpose were to scrutinize us from head to toe, to ensure we were 'modestly' attired for the church service. It was a customary practice in those times. One woman who was sent away for her dress being too short at the front remarked, "I come here to render my heart not my garment." One of the older women at the door replied, "Not as Jezebel! Is shame you ent have so or you don't fear the lord to cover yourself to stand before him! These young people today, no shame! You come here to lure good men from their wives!"

The woman then retorted in frankness, "So you saying when I am in the river bathing I cannot talk to my lord? This church is not for the lord. It is for you and your kind to worship your fears. God loves his children naked or clothed and as a man thinketh low in his heart, so is his soul. Besides, why would I want those men who will put shackles on my feet! My ancestors were not free but I am free today! I am a free woman and no shackles will be put on these feet! You loathers of other women are the vile ones. You don't know God. You know nothing of his love and mercy." She then stormed off angrily.

Her name was Mary Dubois. She was once a school teacher who had been fired and shunned for her unorthodox views. Luckily for her, she was heir to a moderate inheritance which included a house and lands.

Moments later, I saw another woman walk past the older women, with a dress fashioned with the same low cut at the chest, very much similar to the one Mary Dubois was wearing. She sashayed in, cat-like and seductive with provocative sways of her hips; her haircut short at shoulders and uncovered—although it was prohibited—adorned in the finest jewellery and she sat down in the section where all the whites often occupied. I instantly recognized her as the woman who had once given Susan and me a ride home from Sunday school.

It was our first time in an automobile and for days after we recounted the experience. I remember wondering why the trees were moving by so quickly as we sat in the back seat of her automobile. I was mesmerized by the way her hands effortlessly guided the huge steering wheel and how her tiny feet manipulated the brakes and gas, appearing so skilful at what they were doing. I was lost in admiration of a woman driving an automobile and unconsciously wore a smile on my face, because she then commented, "You have a beautiful smile and if you want to keep it, choose love above all else."

Her name was Deirdre Lewis. Her Husband was magistrate Lewis. She came from a poor white Irish family. In those times, to be white, poor and of Irish blood was equivalent to being black. However life had endowed her with mesmerizing beauty and red fiery hair. One of the men who had taken notice of her beauty was magistrate Lewis during one of his regular visits to Jamaica. The middle-aged magistrate then made an offer to her family which would free them from the grasp of poverty and they accepted, and so at the tender age of sixteen she was sent off to Grenada.

She was one of the few whites that often associated with blacks on the island. Maybe she understood what it felt like to be a victim, trapped by one's own physical confines and imprisoned by the thoughts of others. However before Deirdre came to Grenada, she had another life unknown to many, for amidst her family's poverty stricken state she had discovered love. His name was Jean Quinn, the son of a clandestine love union between a white Irish overseer and a black woman. She knew happiness then. In the end, she sold her happiness and broke a man's soul in exchange for a life of luxury. In the end life made sure she learnt her lesson for her cold actions.

A storm on the outside can only affect you if there is a storm on the inside. It is always best to calm the one within you to avoid being affected by the one outside.

8.

Ruth

Growing up I saw many fights. I saw fights between neighbours, fights between Paul and Paulette, fights between my mother and father. Once I had even witnessed a teacher and one of her students scuffling over a man.

Apparently the man was married to the teacher and her student was what we called 'the outside woman'. In the end he left them both for a woman called Paula. Paula was a light-skinned dougla woman who had migrated from St. Lucia. Of course, people said it was because she 'hold him' in callaloo soup, but it was something else, something stronger. In those days colour was what dictated status. In those days nothing mattered more than skin colour and hair texture.

I myself had even been in fights. One time a girl called me 'rum man daughter'. She had done so on many occasions before and I had grown weary of it. When I told my aunt Hazel, she told me what to do. On the following day on the instructions of my aunt, I hid in the bushes and waited for the girl in the short cut which led to her house. As soon as she was close enough to me, I jumped out from my hiding spot and gave her an unsuspecting beating with a piece of stick I had specifically chosen for her, from the big hibiscus tree not too far from my house. She ran away howling as I pursued her bare-footed, discontented with how much lashes I had already given her. However, unknown to me she had the speed of a mongoose crossing the road in the midday sun.

Another time a girl called me 'thin foot' and pulled my hair. Again on the instruction of my aunt, I waited for her in the bushes, but this time I carefully lined up twenty middle-sized stones. Jill was her name. She was of mixed descent—Caucasian and Indian. she was four times my size. I was not taking any chances since she had a reputation for winning fights due to her size. I recall one time Jill and another girl had a heated debate over whose hair was the prettiest in the class. In the end, Jill flung the girl effortlessly across the classroom as a paper jet, leaving behind scattered chairs and tables along the path where she had thrown the girl. Another time she gave a boy a head-butt because he refused to share his lunch with her. The poor boy only responded with tears as she ate the lunch his mother had prepared for him. Jill was a bully in every sense of the word. She was reputed for extortions, provocations and intimidating those around her.

In the end Jill ran off, screaming in shrieks of pain as each one of the stones I had lined up angrily greeted different parts of her body. The next day she appeared with her mother and her three sisters in front my house. All five of them came puffed up, prepared for a fight. My aunt and my mother were not having it. They stood there in silence—inviting the other side to challenge them. Eventually after much lashing of tongue and futile hype, Jill and her gang left. They were too afraid of my aunt and my mother.

The following day was Friday. Apparently Jill's mother was more than determined to seek out revenge for her daughter. As I stood attending to a customer, she intentionally pushed me from the back. I would have fallen on my face had it not been for the woman in front of me. It would be long before Miss Deepa found the courage to sell again in the St. George's Market Square. The beating she received on that day from my mother was as plentiful as rain during a hurricane. My mother was a force not to be reckoned with. Everyone knew that. Jill's mother learnt that day.

However, the fight that remains etched in my mind, was the one which occurred between Ruth and Patricia because no one saw it coming. Ruth was as shy as the very word itself. She rarely spoke to anyone except Liz and me. Patricia and her friends were the class tormentors. On that morning, Patricia called Ruth 'ugly blackie' as she always did but on that fateful day something was different. Ruth was not Ruth at all, and just like that she threw herself onto Patricia and started pounding her face with her fist. Patricia's comrades tried desperately to pull Ruth off but they were thrown in to the corner, one after the other, like crumpled pieces of paper. Ruth was possessed with pure rage and fury. She kept pounding Patricia, until Mr. Ogilvy the science teacher came and pulled her off. Patricia never tormented anyone after that again.

Ruth was suspended for two weeks and was told to return with her parents. Swiftly thereafter, Ruth became the most popular student in our school. On many occasions she took to screaming for extended periods during the school hours. Sometimes it happened in the middle of classes. Sometimes it happened during the break and lunch periods.

Each time, she would start kicking and screaming, "Don't touch me! Don't touch me!" if anyone approached her, and just like that she would stop and assume a trance like form, slowly rocking back and forth with her eyes stuck on one spot, and each time she was sent home for two weeks for bad behaviour.

In response to her bizarre episodes, our principal told her one day in front of the whole class, "I will break you. You will act like a lady." Ruth was no longer a good girl according to the school's standards.

I felt ashamed to be associated with Ruth and so I avoided her as if she was cursed with the black plague itself. Liz on the other hand continued being the loyal friend as always. Then one day Ruth did not attend school and a day turned into days, and days turned into weeks, and weeks turned into a month and still Ruth was not present at school. I was elated to have her gone. I no longer had to worry about being labelled as a delinquent student by association.

Later on in the school term I asked Liz about Ruth. She looked at me in my eyes and scolded, "Why do you care? You are a deep kind of hypocrite, just like some of these teachers here in this school, thinking you know all. Your heart is hollow and you are blind, and just as you are known by the company you keep, you are also known by the company you refuse to keep. Do you know why you always place first in class? You place first because I make sure I leave out some questions on our math exams, so you can have your precious first place. I value our friendship that much. Don't ask me about Ruth, but if you want to know so badly, then you should know she travelled to Trinidad, with a baby in her belly, her uncle's baby!"

She then walked away, leaving me there to swallow it all and it was all too hard to digest.

Ruth is pregnant? How could this happen? Ruth! Her uncle?

Humility and education are synonyms of each other.

9.

Liz

Liz avoided me thereafter—for four weeks she did not speak to me or even look in my direction. If ever I attempted to speak to her she would walk away or stare at me angrily, until I bowed my head in shame and walked away in the other direction. I was beyond devastated.

I felt lost without her presence and guilty because I had abandoned Ruth in her moment of need. I found myself wishing I could return to the past and not care about saving my own reputation. I had a hard time coming to terms with the fact that I had lost my two best friends because I was selfish. I think that was one of my biggest points of reflection as a young girl.

Then one Friday Liz walked up to me and said, "Now you know what it feels like to have someone you love walk away from you." She then hugged me and invited me to her house the following Sunday.

When Sunday finally came, my mother arranged a ride with Mr. Paloma. As I sat in the back of the donkey cart, I busied myself thinking about Liz. She was so many things and yet so simple at the same time. One minute she was this silly school girl, then she would discreetly slip into a dominant personality. I was always giddy with glee when spending time with her, but above all, in Liz's presence I could be myself, my truest self, not the good Mary for school, not the good daughter for my mother, not the good girl for society. I was allowed to be me.

I had never been to Liz's house before. I knew she lived with her father. He was a lawyer. Her mother had ran off with some rich man, Liz once bravely told me.

When I questioned her further, about not having her mother in her life she responded, "My mother birthed me and for that I am grateful to her, for that was her purpose or else she would have stayed. When people are meant to stay, they will stay despite the odds," she continued. On her face emerged a strange look, whether it was a smile or sadness or something else, I could not tell.

I always imagined Liz's house to be elaborate, with maids and at least one motor car outside, since her father was a lawyer. However to my great surprise, here I was standing in front of a neatly built board house, no bigger than my own home, with a small kitchen garden to the side. A man then appeared in the tiny doorway of the house and greeted me. It was Liz's father. It was my first time meeting him, but I instantly remembered seeing him once in the shop, waiting in line for Mr. Rolo to bill up his goods. When he left I overheard a customer mutter, "That man is a communist. What a waste of good education. Some people wish they could have his type of education."

The Rebellion of Mary Magdalene

When I entered Liz's home I instantly fell in love with what I saw. I was in a room filled with books; large books, small books, colourful books, so many books in different sizes and colours. I felt at home.

Right at the top where all the books were kept, carved into the board, were the words: *'The man who reads can question and the one who questions is free; and the one who is free can have endless possibilities.'* I fell in love with those words and they later became the impetus for self-growth.

Later on in the day, while eating the coo-coo with stewed fish and callaloo her father had prepared, Liz told me her father was a lawyer of the 'have-nots'. She then went on to explain the intricate linings of her thoughts. Liz like her father believed in working for the greater good of a community, as opposed to satisfying one's own selfish desires. My perspective on many things changed thereafter.

Liz's father was Grenadian by birth. His mother was a rich Portuguese business woman and his father was a sailor. Through good connections and his almost white skin, he was admitted into a prestigious law school in England and it was there he became exposed to a world of enlightenment.

On my way home in Mr. Paloma's donkey cart, I was lost in a trail of memories from the events of the day and the words of Liz's father, "If education restricts your thoughts and decides your path for you, then it is not education. Every chain has a purpose and our education system is replete with them."

Not all truth free us, some wrap us in chains and throw us at the bottom of the sea, only to become monsters of the sea.

10.

The Letter

We heard the news from the butcher's wife who was very eager to share the latest gossip, about how Mr. McMillan had died peacefully in his sleep. Up until then, the McMillans rarely crossed my mind, not since the event with my sister.

I remember seeing Mr. McMillan from time to time on my way to school. Sometimes, he would be riding his handsome brown horse or passing by in his shiny black automobile, or simply walking. He would always stare at me in the most peculiar manner, as if he knew about the money I had stolen from my mother's purse, as if he knew I was the one who threw stones at Ole Mary when she was taking her bath in the river, as if he knew I blamed him and his family for my sister's death. Whatever his reason was, I made it my duty to hold his stare until he looked away, leaving me feeling victorious.

When the butcher's wife brought the news to us, my aunt did the strangest thing, she fainted and when she returned to her senses, she fainted again. My mother said it was because of the heat. The butcher's wife looked unconvinced but she agreed and offered some advice.

On the day Paul McMillan Sr. was buried, my aunt wore black and shed tears for unknown reasons. She also refused to touch her food and remained in her room without company. In only three weeks, she was half her size and wore a mask of pure misery.

A month after the death of Mr. McMillan a man showed up on our doorstep. I recognized him instantly despite the bushy beard he now sported. He was the man who once taught Sunday school lessons. He was the man responsible for my sister's death. Apparently my mother recognized him too because she flew to the front of the door and shouted, "Get from here you Lucifer, evil and cursed as the womb that bore you!"

Paul McMillan Jr. removed his hat, bowed and contested, "I am sorry ma'am. I know I have caused your family great sadness and because of it, you would rather not wish to see the likes of me. Maybe you even wish to see me confined to the pits of hell for all eternity and if such is the case, I do not blame you. However, I am no longer the coward boy who lived in his mother's shadow. I am a man now and I have accepted the fact that my cowardice led me to betray the one I loved and I destroyed her and brought unbearable pain to your family in the process. I ask for your forgiveness although I know none shall be given nor is it deserved, but I will ask for it despite the odds, and I fear even if by some miracle of God it is granted, it changes nothing, for I shall bear my guilt and my shame for such is my penance and I shall accept no other. I swear by the Almighty, that if I could change the hands of time I would undo it all."

He then cleared his throat as if to regain control of his voice which had started to crack and crumble under notes of remorse and sadness and he said, "I am also here to deliver a letter from my father to your sister. This was to be delivered to her a long time before my father's passing, however my mother saw it fit to prevent such."

He then handed my mother a brown envelope he held in his hand. He bowed courteously for the second time and walked away, his back stiff but yet broken. Something gnawed at my heart and I suddenly felt both pity and sadness for him, as he disappeared from my sight somewhere down the road.

Up until the death of Mr. McMillan, my aunt and I were very close. We spent a lot of time together and she knew the secrets I would not dare reveal to my mother. Like the time I hit Ole Mary with a pebble because I wanted to see her spirits—those she had control over, as people claimed. When the stone hit her on her torso, she turned around and laughed heartily in the direction the stone came from. Another time, I stole one of her chickens and let it free somewhere in the bushes and still no spirits came for me. I was disappointed and relieved. My aunt who was a strong believer in the supernatural looked at me as if air was suddenly removed from her body when I told her. She made me promise to desist from provoking

Ole Mary. Of course, I made the promise and I broke it soon after.

As my mother handed the letter to my aunt, she muttered, "Let it die sister. May the past be buried. Let it die." My aunt then started sobbing while my mother repeated again in a sombre tone, "Let it die."

I heard all this while eavesdropping and peeping in the corner of the door to my aunt's room. That night my mind was racing with many questions. What was in the letter? How did my aunt know Mr. McMillan? I felt like walking into her room and demanding the truth from my aunt but I knew my mother would punish me severely, so I stayed awake trying to find answers to the questions in my head, to no avail though.

The following day was Sunday, church day for my family. I was in the middle of a beautiful dream running through rows and rows of beautiful flowers of all colours—red, yellow, pink, white, blue, violet and many more—when my aunt woke me up and told me she wanted to speak to me. We were the only ones in the house. Everyone else had left for church. The night before, I was instructed to stay at home and watch over my aunt since she insisted on maintaining her peculiar behaviour.

"Mammy said to make sure you eat something today," I mumbled between sleep and wake.

Sitting on the chair next to my bed she smiled and said, "You have grown into such a beautiful and smart young lady, so intelligent, so beautiful," she wept. She then got up, turning her back to me while gazing out the window and began her story.

"When I was seventeen I came to Grenada from Trinidad with the intention of staying and making a life for myself. I wanted to become a nurse. I also missed my sister and wanted to see her again. When Cecilia and I were girls, we were inseparable despite our age difference. My intention was never to fall in love." She then turned around and looked at me and continued, "Yes I fell in love and never recovered and now I am dying of the very thing that once brought me the greatest joy."

She then handed me the letter and emotions never felt before flowed through me as I read the content. What I was reading could not be true!

My aunt studied me and as if she read my thoughts she added, "It is true baby girl. It is true."

That was the last thing she said before she collapsed at the side of the bed. At first I stared at her body on the ground, too stunned to move, my mind trying to wrap itself around the letter and my aunt's motionless body on the floor. Somehow, I was able to free myself from the trance and I managed to get Dr. Thomas to our house. High blood pressure was the cause of death.

On the day aunt Hazel was buried rain fell for the entire day and late into the night too. Many people came to her funeral, even Mr. Ching came all the way from Trinidad to pay his respects. In a thick Chinese accent he said, "Hazel, nice girl. Hazel work hard. Hazel makes all customers happy." He then bowed and left.

If you play a theme too long, it becomes an anthem and some themes should never become anthems.

11.

The Rebellion of Mary Magdalene

The following year I entered form 4 and was appointed class prefect. I was not enthusiastic about the idea, unlike my mother who seemed all too thrilled and boasted to the neighbours that her daughter was a prefect.

I hated it instantly. I was constantly supervising the girls in my class and in turn was expected to be in constant supervision of my own behaviour. It was a simple control tactic to keep me and the other girls in line.

One Friday our English teacher gave us an assignment to write on someone of our own choosing who changed the course of history. At that time Liz and I had mastered the art of clean competition. We studied together and we excelled together at school and we were both happy when either of us got the highest on a test. Sometimes Liz got the highest. Sometimes I got the highest. Sometimes we got the same score.

I remember Liz's father saying, "The very genesis of man is a competitive one. Man must learn to use this natural characteristic to achieve that which they say he cannot achieve, to conquer his own doubts. There is no growth in looking at others and trying to match others. If you compete with someone else they will always be the victor, for time wasted on them could have been spent on your own evolution."

On Monday morning we were all asked to read our essays aloud, one by one. When it was my turn I got up and read aloud the following:

The Rebellion of Mary Magdalene

I have chosen to write about one of the most famous women in history and yet for all little is written about her person. I have chosen this woman because I think she is an embodiment of our society today. I have chosen to write about none other than Mary Magdalene, the heroine of her time and my time. It is my belief that through her remembrance, light will drive away the darkness that covers our eyes and hearts on this small island.

Have you ever wondered who Mary Magdalene was? Not the Sunday school stories of her, but her person. For example, who named her? Was it her mother? Or was it her father? What was she like growing up? Did she have a hard life, a good life? Did she have a good heart? What were her aspirations? What was her contribution to society? I ask these questions not for a response, but for us to reflect and of course we do not know the answers. My point exactly! Nothing is recorded except for her supposed crime. Her person was erased by this supposed crime. How fair is it, to be remembered only for a crime?

Moreover, I hereby call her accomplice to the stand to face trial for his part in the crime; for if indeed she did commit such a crime, then there must have been an accomplice. Where was he? Was he in the group that was about to stone her? Or was he at home as I suspect, without a care in the world? I call him to stand trial as Mary did. She was subjected to humiliation and the threat of death, so where were you accomplice? Come out you coward! Come out and be subjected to the same fate that Mary endured.

I also call to trial her accusers. Where was her accomplice to the crime you were about to stone her for? Could you not see the unfairness in your attempted prosecution? What are your own crimes, accusers? Tell us so we can judge you accordingly, for even if it is hidden, a crime remains true to its nature, still a crime. Tell us your own crimes accusers! Let us judge you as you have judged Mary. Tell us about your crimes, the ones committed in utmost secrecy and the ones that lurk in your heart, for after-all there are no angels among us. Tell us your own crimes! We will like to render the same service of judgement! We will like to render the same service of judgement! We will like to render the same service of judgement!

I also call to trial, the women of Mary Magdalene's time. Where were you women as Mary was made to endure this walk of shame and possible death? Did you not see the hypocrisy that was before you? Did you not look at her and see a reflection of yourselves, that men always defend the ills of men, reserving prosecution only for women?Could you not feel her pain? Or did your own molded and well fed insecurity in your own beauty made you see Mary as a threat, and thus stoning her became necessary?

Furthermore, I also call to trial the men of our society. Yes, the men in this society. How many of us know a girl who had to leave school, to travel to Trinidad to deliver a baby to hide the shame? How many of us know a girl or woman who had to go to Ole Sandra, to destroy a part of her because of fear? How many girls do you know who are forced to carry the 'shame' of rape brought upon her, sometimes by the hands of her very own blood; her father, an uncle, a grandfather? How many of us know a mother who is raising her grandchild as her own to hide the so called shame of her daughter? How many women do you know who are scorned for being the other woman? Is it not true that a crime of such nature has two accomplices? So why do we point a finger to one only?

I call to trial the women of our time also. Why do you sit by in silence and allow men to crucify your daughters, oppress us, restrict us to only childbearing and the kitchen, as if that is all we are capable of? Why do you partake in such a treacherous act with your silence? Why is it that when a so called crime is committed, we women are always the ones to throw the first stone, to make the first hurtful remark? And her person, her aspiration, her contribution becomes invalid and thus she is remembered and branded as a criminal by her own sisters.

Are we not supposed to be our sisters' keepers? You have failed your sisters! As the women of Mary's time, you have broken the sacred trust of sisterhood. Oh mothers, you have failed us! Oh sisters, you have failed us! Society has boxed us in and equipped us with claws and venom, to use against each other as we fight over this single title of 'good girl'. While distracted by this illusion, they prey on us. There are no good girls' and there are no 'bad girls'. We are just women and we are stronger and capable of more than the weak and passive roles they have subjected us to. Wake up!

Morality! Morality! Morality! I question thee also!

You shackle me morality. You oppress me morality! Free me morality! Free me! Free me!

I question that which we have been made to believe is morality. What is this morality and should it not be fair? Morality is fair! Morality is fair! It should serve everyone for his or her own betterment. When men use laws for their own vices, it is no longer morality. It is oppression and for far too long they have been educating us, not to free us, but to cage us, to remove our wings, so that we can become earthly things.

This is me! This is you! This is us! These are things we see and know because we live it every day. Yes, we are the modern day Mary Magdalene. They throw stones at us, weigh us down with unjustified guilt and shame. They brand us like cattle; our hopes, our dreams, our contribution to society gone in the wind and history would write us down for our crimes in the end. Now, is that fair? And the hypocrisy of it all, it is only we and we alone who are made to stand trial, while our accomplices are given free passes to move on to the next.

My sisters as all of you know, my name is Mary Moses and I think it is fate itself I have the name Mary, the first name of our heroine, the lady of truth and light.

Viva Maria Magdalena!!!!!!

When I finished I took my seat, but the girls in my class did not let it end there. They started pounding their desks and applauding, as if they had in their heads those very same sentiments and were simply waiting for someone to say it. They began pounding the desks as if they no longer regarded the consequences of such unfeminine conduct, for 'little girls are seen and not heard'—but we were no longer little girls, we were young women yearning for freedom, being called to rebellion. We were Mary and Mary was us.

It took four teachers to quiet us down but something was different thereafter. We saw ourselves not in the image which they had taught us, but in the image of Mary Magdalene, our heroine. We were Mary and Mary was us.

I was sent home for two weeks for inciting 'unruly unladylike behaviour'.

"You should be ashamed. You are a prefect!" my principal shrieked, as she handed me the letter.

In my head and with my unregretful demeanour, I answered her back, 'I am not your slave driver. I will not run your slave plantation. I am Mary! I will not bow to your hypocrisy.'

My mother refused to speak to me for an entire week. This time the letter sent home to her was a rather lengthy one. It seemed as if it took her forever to read. In all honesty at that point I made no reservation for her feelings and neither did I care about the lies Miss Jacob had concocted in that letter, for I could have easily read it but I was tired with lies. I hungered for the truth.

The Rebellion of Mary Magdalene

Mr. Bishop had once told me, "You are not ready for the truth or change, if you are not ready to sacrifice for it."

I was ready to sacrifice for it.

•••

The events which followed on the Monday I returned to school was the beginning of many things, for I was now seeing small things as giants and big things as ant-like. As I mounted the short stairs that lead to the classroom, my feet grew heavier with each step. I could hear my mother's voice echoing in my head, "good girls conform". The word conform and the meaning of conformity were stuck in my brain, feeling around blindly, trying to fully create a meaning.

When I got to the front of the classroom, Miss Jacob glared at me. I smiled at her in return. She seemed astonished but pleased with my response and her face took on an air of victory. I stood there, all eyes on me. They were all wearing the same costume—the air ripe with anticipation. As I looked at my fellow sisters my tongue suddenly became tangled and refused to move. My heart galloped in the deafening silence and my throat suddenly became dry and parched, as the land during the dry season, dry like the time I had killed a lizard and got dry skin because of it, according to my mother.

I hesitated for a while. I closed my eyes, steadied my courage and then out of my mouth came these words to the anticipating audience before me:

"The day you become less of them and more of you, you will achieve your greatest potential. Dare to be different, for it is difference that brought forth the world from the stone ages. Someone said, instead of using a stick, I will make a hoe and the magic happened. Don't worry about the critics, their job is as such. Salute to the modern day heretics, burn us at the stake, throw us in the gallows and we shall be reborn only to be the phoenix."

I then turned to Miss Jacob who was now draped in a raging pink and I declared, "I owe you no apology, for it is you who should apologize for trying to kill my voice; for it is you who should apologize for trying to impose the vice of hypocrisy on us. You are a hypocrite. You are modern day slave master whipping us into submission. I stand in the image of Mary Magdalene. I am reborn and I am saved, saved from your hypocrisy!"

As I walked down the stairs, I heard the first spate of applause. Then I heard a second, then many more joined in and it was pure chaos. The girls from my class started chanting, "Long live Mary Magdalene! Long live Mary Magdalene! Long live Mary Magdalene!"

The girls from the other classes looked on as my classmates displayed a terrifying form of rebellion and defiance they had never witnessed before. I saw Liz pounding a table with her fist. I saw Patricia doing the same. Some girls removed their ties and waved it in the air, as if was it was carnival. Jane, the new girl who never spoke and always kept her hair in a bun, removed her shirt and was beating a table with the rod used to scold us whenever we got out of hand. It was the same stick Mr. Phillip had scorched my back with during a math period, when I had turned around to borrow Jane's Pencil. Jane always had many pencils and on that day my pencil was nowhere to be found—a cruel prank by my brother Paul.

The air was richly saturated with the smell of liberation, and conservatism was in a state of panic. It took the teachers a good hour or more, to quiet the girls down. In the end, we were all sent home with notes. An emergency meeting was to be held with our parents the following day.

The following day was exactly as I imagined it—parents filled the room. They were informed of my actions and I was singled out as the instigator of 'malicious heathen behaviour' according to Miss Jacob. Out of the corner of my eyes I could see my mother bowing her head—in shame I assumed, as I was demonized by the principal. I could read the other parents' thoughts. In their heads I was a bad influence, a weed in a promising garden. They wanted me rooted out. However, there was one parent who thought differently—Liz's father, Mr. Bishop. He had listened attentively to our principal like the other parents then his turn to speak arrived.

"Do you have a copy of the essay that was written, the 'evil literature' you speak of?" he asked politely, but firm.

Miss Jacob was stunned by this unforeseen question. Miss Jacob then replied, "Such an essay was destroyed. We have a standard to maintain here."

Mr. Bishop responded, "Not a problem because I have a copy. You see, I know this child very well and I was well informed of the events that have us all here today. I think that Mary is nothing or not even close to what you have described. In fact she is a child with questions and questions are normal."

He then read my essay aloud to the other parents, afterwards commenting, "I see no problems with this essay. There are no lies in here. There is no act of rebellion. There are no heathen themes here either. This is an essay which simply expresses sentiments towards a social injustice and you as a woman should understand this well. Yes, the girls disrupted classes but that blame rest on us, because we have never given them the power nor chance to voice their opinions. I do not think this child should be made to suffer for her act of bravery, and it is indeed brave to ask such questions in a society as ours. If these things were discussed and addressed outrightly then this would have never happened. We live in a society where men prey on women and women are told to stay quiet about it."

In the end some parents agreed with him while some did not. I was punished with two weeks suspension while the other girls received detention.

At home my mother refused to speak to me or even look in my direction. On the second day of my suspension, I waited until we were alone and I handed her the letter my aunt had given me on the day she died. I had hidden it beneath my bed, on the day my aunt had passed away, silently watching as my mother frantically searched all over the house for it, while pretending she was searching for something else.

Kissandra Smith

My beloved Hazel,

Where do I begin? Where do I end? There are so many things I wish to say, but what good are they now? I have hurt you in the most cruellest of ways, shamed you, betrayed you, brought pain into your life. I beg for your forgiveness. I beg you.

I have written to you so many times, but you never replied, and I understand why you chose not to. I have lived a lavish life that many have wished for, while I was wishing for theirs, for in theirs, I would have had more courage. I would have fought for us.

I now look at the things that I chose over you; money, family name and a wife who only loves my money and her image, an unhappy marriage. My heart bleeds with regret. If I could give it up now for you, I would be rich beyond measure, because you are indeed a treasure, the most beautiful one, the kindest one.

After all these years these eyes that can no longer see, still see you. After all these years, these ears that have failed me, can still hear the music in your laughter.

At my bedside my only friend is Dr. Thomas. I often wonder where all the friends I had chosen over you have disappeared to. How could I have been so stupid to give up on true love for the sake of reputation?

My dearest Hazel, a day has not passed that you are not in my thoughts. I still love you. An old man in love? Yes an old man still in love with his soul mate. You will always be the light of my soul. I pray God reunites us in the next life. I pray he does, for without you in the heaven He has promised us, it will indeed be my hell.

I understand why you did what you did. I understand you needed to protect her from her father's ugliness. I know that Mary Moses is my daughter. I know you gave her to your sister to raise as her own.

On so many occasions I wanted to walk up to her and hug her and tell her the truth, but I think it is fair that you should be the one, if ever, to reveal this precious secret. A father knows his child and she is my child. I pray that you tell her. I pray that you bring her to my bedside before I die. I pray. Give me the chance to beg for her forgiveness. Give me the opportunity to ask for a chance in her heart. My dying wish is that you grant me this one wish.

With love
Paul McMillan Sr.

Some of the strongest bonds exist between siblings.

12.

Paul and Paulette

When I was in form 1, my brother Paul was in form 5. When I got to form 3, he had long completed his secondary schooling and was working with my mother in the garden.

Paulette, unlike Paul and I, never attended secondary school, for she had her fair share of struggles. She often had difficulties in differentiating certain letters of the alphabet. Thus, spelling words that others deemed easy proved to be a mountainous task for her. However, Paulette could solve a math problem on the drop of a hat and she was also a talented artist—so intricate and enchanting were her paintings, that once an English gentleman who was visiting the island bought five of her paintings. Of course, she was paid almost next to nothing; just enough to buy a week's worth of candies perhaps, for failure of knowing one's worth is indeed a tragedy.

I remember our little house being adorned with all these paintings, showcasing the vibrant colours and vigour of our beautiful Grenada. Paulette was indeed a paragon of a gifted person, all of which went unnoticed since the education system was not designed to accommodate those who differed from the standard — those who had a phenomenal aptitude for being artistic.

In turn the teachers showed her no patience. In retaliation she showed the teachers no respect for their attitude towards her. One day a teacher called her a 'dunce bat' and Paulette in heightened vexation and embarrassment, told her something to the effect that her resemblance was striking to a pregnant sow. Paulette was then sent to the principal, who sided with the teacher. In response, a frustrated Paulette gave the principal a good tongue lashing. As a result she was dismissed from school with no possibility of re-entry.

In the end, my mother sent Paulette to learn the art of sewing by a local seamstress and she excelled at it. Sometimes the closing of one door leads to the opening of the one we are destined to walk through.

"She has a calling for it," the seamstress lady told my mother once.

When I burnt my school skirt, Paulette helped me sew a new one. When I intentionally burnt Paul's school pants and was frightful after, she stitched it up nicely for me.

Paulette, Paul and I had an unbreakable bond since we were all familiar with the pain of losing a sibling. So when Paulette fell in love with Robert, she told Paul and me about him, but it was I who became her confidant during that time. She told me that Robert was from the other side of the island and that he had moved to St. David with his mother and father for reason of employment.

However, naive Paulette madly in love with Robert, neglected the fact that he always had an excuse for not wanting to meet Paul and me; or him insisting their story should be kept between them; or that he never took her to social gatherings and even the fact, that he pretended not to know her in public.

I disliked Robert instantly just from the stories Paulette told. Of course, I kept this all to myself. I was of age to understand that a woman in love is sometimes a fool in love and no words could break such a spell. So I sat each time and with a heavy heart and a restrained tongue, I listened to stories about Robert and I wiped Paulette's tears on the days he made her cry and I comforted her on the days when the truth she did not have the courage to acknowledge, lurked in her soul. Robert did not love Paulette. Paulette was in love with her own imagination.

Then one beautiful Wednesday morning, a girl came into the seamstress store to take her measurements for her wedding dress. A conversation started up and the girl revealed she was going to marry her soul mate by the name of Robert. She further revealed that they had been dating for a while now, and he treated her like a queen and took her out to the fancy places. This Robert turned out to be Paulette's very own Robert, the one she had blindly surrendered her heart and soul to.

At first, Paulette told herself it was a case of mistaken identity, for Robert was quiet and respectable and would never do such a thing. Then one day while on her way home from work, she took a different route and there he was, Robert. He was not alone. He was sitting cosily with the girl. They were busy laughing and talking, holding hands, eyes locked in a romantic embrace. It was indeed a beautiful scene to any onlooker but for Paulette it sliced her heart open and her world came crashing down.

When confronted with the question he did not deny it and offered no apology either. Instead he turned on Paulette and told her he owed her nothing and that he did not love her and he was going to marry the other girl. Apparently this girl was Robert's ideal catch—an affluent family with many connections and a girl of mixed race—half Lebanese, half Indian. Later on he would replace this girl with another and replace the other with another and so he went on, until life grew tired of hearing the cries of women.

Paulette then took a trip to Ole Sandra. It was this secret that solidified our bond even further; for pain and sadness sometimes have a way of moulding human beings together.

My job was to accompany her to Ole Sandra's house. My job was also to tell my mother that Paulette would be spending the night in the seamstress shop to finish someone's wedding dress—it was a lie of course. Robert never knew; he had threatened to tarnish Paulette's reputation if she ever told anyone about their past relationship.

Some of Robert's words to Paulette were, "I was never with you. There was never anything between us and there will never be anything between us. Ask yourself Paulette, did you ever feel loved by me, then why did you stay? I kept you at a great distance for a reason. I never loved you, stupid girl—and don't even think about telling your mother about me, for no one will make me marry you and besides wait until I tell everyone that good ole church girl, 'singing in the church choir Paulette' is a bad girl. You are a fallen girl Paulette. Didn't the good Pastor Newton tell you to keep your legs closed until you are wed? Tell anyone about us and I will expose you. I am getting married next month and I better not hear one single word about us, or else. Look at you crying! Pathetic and weak, I despise you weak women. Stop crying! I did not force you to be with me Paulette! Stop crying! You did this to yourself! You really thought I would marry you!"

I overheard all this while sitting in the seamstress shop waiting for my sister. It was customary for the owner to leave the shop in Paulette's care from time to time. I still remember the way I felt after overhearing this man talk so vilely to my sister, my dear sister, my beloved Paulette. It was as if sadness had reached out and consumed my very own heart in one bite.

Robert was one of the wicked men of whom our mother had warned us about—a misogynist. My mother used to say, "Men take, men hurt, men destroy and they ride off into the sunset with your heart. Protect your hearts." Robert did not ride off into the sunset with

Paulette's heart. Instead he stabbed it, mutilated it and left Paulette for dead.

•••

To this very day I never knew how Paul found out about Robert's actions towards Paulette, but he did. When Paul confronted Robert, a fight quickly resulted. Robert's wife, heavy under the influence of his deceptive charms used all her 'family links' to ensure Paul was arrested, although it was Robert who had thrown the first punch. Paul was sent to Her Majesty's Prison for two years. The charges laid before him were assault on an officer and attempted murder of a man, both of which were false. The news broke my mother and it broke Paulette, for she blamed herself.

Paul was an alpha male. He believed in protecting women and those who lacked the power to defend themselves. I remember one time we were returning home from the market and a man was beating his wife with a cutlass. Paul rushed in and gave the man a taste of his own medicine with the same cutlass—across his back, across his pot belly and his head, just as he had done to the woman. Then there was this other time a boy threw curse words in my direction because I refused to entertain his weak flattery—Timmon was his name. Paul gave him such a bad beating that the boy would cross the street every time he saw me. On the other hand, Paul would see two men fighting or quarrelling and he would turn away in the other direction. He was also very good with children and he loved animals.

When he was released from prison he moved in with Paulette, who by that time owned her own seamstress shop and house. She had clients from all over. One of them became a suitor and they later married sometime after Paul's release.

Paul was taken on as an apprentice by Paulette's husband, who was a successful large scale farmer and in the span of a year, Paul had saved up enough to start his own farming venture. Eventually he married a girl from St. Lucia and they had three beautiful children. Paulette on the other hand gave birth to seven children—four boys and three girls.

I was in form 3 when Paul was sentenced to two years imprisonment. I watched as my brother was carried away in chains—sadness and anger boiling together in his eyes. I was in form 3 when I watched my sister cry, as she drank the portion Ole Sandra had mixed for her. I was in form 3 when I watched her cry as her body expelled that which she wanted to keep but could not keep, for society would cast her away as one of the girls who had fallen from grace. I was in form 3 when I nursed Paulette back to health, both physically and mentally.

Form 3 was the year I finally started seeing the world for what it was, people for who they were and I no longer felt afraid.

Kissandra Smith

Life's letter to Robert

I bind you
I bind you
I bind you
I bind you, not of my own doing, but of yours
I bind you from hurting my daughters
I bind you from hurting the children I have given to you
I bind you
And now father wind will decide your fate
You are not of my sons
You are not of my sons
I bind you

Love is a powerful force, it has broken many and it has made many.

13.

Truth Revealed

I sat there looking at my mother, the woman who sacrificed so much for me, the woman I loved dearly. I think at that point she knew I was far gone from the little girl she had raised. I wanted answers and would accept nothing else.

She said, "Even if I had picked you up from the sea shore, you will still be my daughter and I will always love you."

"Just tell me the truth!" I implored.

The time had come for the truth. I could feel a storm raging within me.

She then began her story, "A long time ago when I was your age, I fell in love. So deeply in love I was willing to sacrifice my education and my family and that is what I did. One day my friends and I decided to visit the wharf and there I met the man you thought was your father. I loved him with every fibre of my being. He had big dreams. He wanted to see the world. He wanted to travel the world and open his own business. I fell in love with his dreams because I too dreamt of those things. However, he was the kind who was filled with dreams and ambitions but lacked the courage to see it through—he was so fearful of failure that he stopped trying. I saw that too late of course. I cannot say I loved him later on in our marriage, but I can say I loved him in the beginning.

"Hazel and I were born to Chandra and George Charles. They were well known in our parts. My father was a businessman who owned a grocery shop, among other small business ventures in San Fernando. He had risen from walking barefooted and working alongside indentured servants for a meagre salary, to a man whom people respected. He was one of those few and fortunate blacks to rise from the hard labour of cutting sugar cane in the smoldering Trinidadian heat. He even married a mixed woman to show it. We lived in a big house and had two maids.

"I can say that my father was capable of love but he never showed it. He was harsh and unbending towards my sister and me and more so to our mother whose temperament was always a docile one. As an esteemed member of our community, strict rules were laid out for Hazel and me. Our life was limited to home and school and talking to boys was strictly forbidden. I was determined to fight him in whatever way I could. I wanted to be free of him, free of the house, free of his many rules, free of the way he treated my mother, free of it all. I just wanted to be free. Life had given him no free passes and he was a man broken in many places, but as a child all I could see was him trying to deprive me of freedom.

"So I fell in love with Ravi Moses and dreamt while he told me about his dreams. He came from a good family. He was of mixed heritage—Indian and African. His father was a doctor and his brother was on his way to becoming a doctor also.

"Then I became pregnant when I was in secondary school. I was not afraid to tell my father, to ruin his dream of seeing me become a nurse. I saw this as my way to finally hurt him and to be free of him. I expected him to shout and hit me as he usually did but he only looked at me with a sadness I will always remember. Three days later he suffered a stroke. He survived but wanted nothing to do with me and then the arguments started between my mother and me. She blamed me for almost ruining our family and now as I look back, I cannot say I blame her. I ruined what my father had worked so hard to build—respect for himself and for his family.

"So I left and boarded a boat with Ravi to Grenada. When we got to Grenada, we moved from house to house at first as Ravi did small jobs to feed us, but the money was never enough to provide. He became more frustrated each day and eventually sank into despair. Eventually I found work and I was able to provide for our family. I built a home for our family from scrubbing floors and washing clothes.

"One Friday night I heard a knock on the door. It was Hazel, she had found me. Mamma had passed away. She told me that in her dying breath mamma had asked for me and said she had forgiven me and gave me her blessings. Only the good lord knows how much I had prayed for my parents' forgiveness. However, papa still wanted nothing to do with me.

"When Hazel told me she wanted to stay, I used my connections to get her a job at the McMillans' mansion as a maid and it was there she began her love affair with Paul McMillan Sr. I tried to stop her but she never listened to me. One day Mrs. McMillan who was very keen on the affairs of her household cornered Hazel and asked her about the affair. When she could not answer, Mrs. McMillan confirmed her suspicion.

"On the following Sunday at an annual dinner party, Mrs. McMillan called the attention of the guests and announced, 'This nigger told me that she is sleeping with my Paul. I overheard her saying it to my cook, and then when I asked her, she then boldly confessed. Is that not so Cynthia?'

"Cynthia was paid extra money to corroborate Mrs. McMillan's story. Paul McMillan Sr. feeling embarrassed and suddenly hot beneath his suit, started calling Hazel the most unmentionable names known to women. His friends and Mrs. McMillan laughed as Hazel ran to the kitchen. Paul McMillan was compelled by force to laugh in order to save face, but in his heart he was dying. Hazel was then fired.

"By then you were a month old inside of her. So she hid indoors for eight months and I pretended to be pregnant. I managed to convince my friend Dr. Thomas to help with the fabrication of your birth. A little while after you were born Hazel left for Trinidad. The pain of seeing the man who betrayed her was too much."

My mother then got up from the old chair and proceeded into her room. She came back with a well folded package. She then handed me the package and said, "I regret doing many things, and this is one of them. I wanted so badly to protect my sister from harm that I did her an injustice, a grave injustice. I cannot ask her for forgiveness but I can ask her child, the daughter I have grown to love as my own. I pray you forgive me."

The package contained letters from my biological father to my biological mother. In each and every one of the letters Paul McMillan Sr. professed his undying love for the woman I grew up calling my aunt. There were endless letters. For years he delivered letters to my mother with the expectation it would reach her sister. They never did. He had found out about me when I was eight years old. Dr. Thomas, his only true friend and confidant felt he needed to know the truth.

I was the daughter of Paul McMillan Sr. I was born from a love story that was robbed of its youth. It left me confused and angry.

If you yearn to open your eyes, one day it will open and never close again.

14.

Ole Mary

On the Friday of the second week of my suspension from school, I paid a visit to the river. I always enjoyed sitting in the shade of the large 'sandbox' trees by the river. It was my favourite past time. I enjoyed watching the water dance between each rock with a smooth agility and swiftness, while creating beautiful harmonic sounds that brought a trance like calmness to any listener.

I was musing when a voice declared, "Ah, the one that loves to throw stones when I am bathing. Don't you want to steal my chickens today? The chicken you stole is back in its cage, for anything that is mine, is forever mine, and every stone that is thrown in my direction, will point me to the hand that was stupid enough to throw it."

It was Ole Mary. She glared at me. Her piercing blue eyes anchored to the depth of my soul as if to challenge me; her very own soul beckoning me to match the fierceness of her mesmerizing knowing abyss-like stare.

Our eyes were locked together for what seemed as an eternity, until I found the courage to utter, "I am not afraid of you, crazy woman!"

She then laughed a big hearty laugh and then her face turned serious and she said, "You are stupid like your father—stupid like white Mr. McMillan. He thought he knew everything," and as if she read my mind from my puzzled look she added, "yes I knew your father, your real father, and like I said, like father like daughter, stupid to the very core."

Although I did not know Mr. McMillan in the way of a father, I suddenly felt the urge to defend him. I then walked up to Ole Mary and I hissed, "Don't speak ill of my father."

She contested by moving even closer to me with the agility and grace of a lioness stalking its prey. We were then face to face with each other when she said, "Do not push me to anger child. I will unleash something so powerful on you, that your children's children and ten generations after will tremble in fear when they hear my name."

Something in her eyes made me believe she was capable of doing such. Then she scolded, "You ungrateful child! Who was the one to remove that evil spirit Mrs. McMillan had sent for you?" and again as if she read my thoughts she added, "It was Mrs. McMillan who sent that evil spirit to kill you, when she finally learnt her husband had fathered a child who would inherit half of his legacy upon his death—an evil art she had learnt while growing up in Martinique. It was through this practice she had summoned the forces to get Mr. McMillan to marry her in the first instance, and when I told him about his coming death by her hands, he chased me away saying, 'God created man only.' I told him, 'God created many things. Man is just one of them, and just because our human eyes cannot see them, that does not mean that they are not there.' In the end his wife saw that he paid for wounding her ego." Ole Mary then turned and started walking in the direction of her hut asking, "Are you coming?"

A mixture of curiosity and uncertainty seized me as my famished eyes scanned Ole Mary's hut. The inside was an intimidating reflection of the outside. The room we entered was small and dimly lit by two kerosene lamps situated in the middle of the room, on the board floor. It housed a single narrow bed, a rattan chair and a grand variety of herbs hung in the middle from the rafters of the hut. There was also a table with bottles which I assumed contained portions. On each bottle were mesmerizing labels written in beautiful calligraphy, but I could not understand 'head nor tail'of it since the language was not English. In time, I would come to write and speak this language, for it was indeed my stolen mother tongue — stolen from my original mother and father when they were 'brought over' and told they could not read and write.

Then there was another thing which caught my eyes, the bookshelf, and the big book, and suddenly the memories of that night came flooding in. I was in the room again, sick, going from hot to cold; the pain that ran all over my body was there again, a thickness permeated the air, death was about to claim me.

"Come this way!" snapped a voice, pulling out of the self-inflicted trance. It was Ole Mary. She pushed past the bookshelf which opened to a secret passage and to my greatest surprise, it led to a much wider space.

Ole Mary's hut was a cave in disguise! A cave neatly hidden away from the world. The interior was replete with books of every size—big ones, bigger ones than the big ones, middle sized ones, bigger middle sized ones, small ones, smaller ones, all neatly packed away on shelves on one side of the room. The floor of the room was nothing but bare hard brown flat rock. Slow burning candles lined the four walls of rock, in box-like shallow spaces carved out for that purpose. On the walls were visible drawings depicting men and animals in stick like forms, as if drawn by a child's imaginative fingers. As my own fingers, ripe and greedy with curiosity traced the outlines of the drawings, it dawned on me that the drawings were indeed storylines.

In a friendly voice Ole Mary explained, "These drawing tell stories of the people who inhabited the island before the Europeans came. This dwelling was once home to a warrior queen of immense courage; the first wife of the last *Ouboutou* who lived on the island. She fought and died alongside her husband during one of the many battles between the invaders and her people. It was said that because of her ferocious fighting skills her enemies cowered whenever her name was mentioned. Even the men of her village knew all too well not to cross her path. She was indeed a great warrior and when she died her children told her story, until it reached my mother, who had been told by her mother.

"In my veins run the blood of a Kalinago man and a runaway African woman. Their story was long lived but long gone. We who know their story sing their names; Aissatou as she was named by her mother and Tiburon, one of the last of his people."

She proceeded to remove her headscarf and from beneath it cascaded short curly black hair. She then washed the cracked mud mask from her face in a large calabash which was filled with crystal clear water. There before me stood a mesmerizingly beautiful woman, so beautiful she evenly matched my mother's undying beauty everyone spoke about.

How old was Ole Mary? She had to be older than Mr. Paloma. She must have been, because the old man had told us he knew Ole Mary since he was a boy and he was probably nearing sixty, but the woman revealed before me now, looked as if she was just nearing thirty.

Either Ole Mary was a mind reader or maybe my puzzled face caused her to reply, "I would have been called Christophine Moses if my mother had registered my birth, but there is no record of my birth just as there is none of my mother's or her mother before her. My father's name was Ravi Moses. You knew him. You once called him father. A long time ago he took refuge here on many occasions to hide away from the cold bitter reality of this world. One thing lead to the next and here I am. My mother birthed me inside this cave and kept me a secret from the world, as her mother did before, and as my great-grandmother did before, as all the other Marys that ever lived here.

"My mother told me and taught me everything I needed to know. I have never left this island but I have travelled through my books. I have revisited the past. I have seen the future. When my mother died I continued our family's tradition as would my daughter, and all Marys give birth to Marys. We never give birth to sons, only daughters, strong daughters. We rise when the occasion requires us to. We break chains. we restore order. we set things right. Freedom is to soul as soul is to freedom. Yes, we make things right. A time will come when you will understand."

...

For the entire school term of form 4, I rotated all my extra time between Old Mary's hut and Liz's house. I had developed an insatiable thirst for knowledge and the truth. Christophine Moses was very versed in the history which was not taught in school. She told me about Queen Nzinga of Angola, Queen Nefertiti of Egypt; Mansa Musa of Mali and the great university of Timbuktu, King Hannibal—the great military strategist of Tunis and many others. It was as if I had finally found my place in the world. She knew about Plato and Aristotle. She knew about ancient civilizations that even the teachers in my school knew nothing about. She tossed light upon the darkened truth about men like John Hawkins and Walter Raleigh. I now had two mentors, Christopine Moses better known as Ole Mary and Mr. Bishop.

I will never forget something Ole Mary said, "Never let them tell you we came from nothing. We had empires and those parts that did not have empires, had structure and organization. Then they came and pillaged and wreaked havoc, disrupted the African evolution—fathers torn from wives, mothers from children and brothers from sisters. We had structure girl! We had languages. We were learned—we could read and write. We knew ourselves and never let them tell you that the abolitionist got us freedom. We were going to sweep this whole part of the world with our burning desire for freedom, but they saw us coming and concocted a plan to calm the situation. If a man gives you a plum you will be forever in his debt, but when you take a plum from a man, power rests in your own hands."

She then continued, "In my homeland, we wore our masks and spoke the Mende language. We had many respected names but here we are just Ole Marys, but we do our jobs nonetheless." She then whispered the last line again while staring into the depth of my soul, "We are just Ole Marys, but we do our jobs nonetheless."

To fight for your person is brave. To fight for others is courageous. One comes from instinct and the other from the depth of the soul.

15.

Raul

Raul was the son of magistrate Lewis. Magistrate Lewis was known for his harsh sentencing of people of African descent. The first time I saw magistrate Lewis was not in the courtroom but on his veranda.

One day while walking home from school, I saw Raul standing next to the old abandoned building school children often used as a playground. He did not appear surprised to see me, and what he did remains engraved in my mind even to this day. He exposed himself to me. I remember running as fast as my little legs could carry me. I remember him chasing after me saying, "I just want to talk to you."

When I got home I immediately told my mother about Raul's vile action. With her cutlass in her right hand and her other hand squeezing my wrist, she angrily marched up to the Lewises' house. I remember her raising the cutlass to Raul's neck, the sun bouncing of the shiny silver end. I remember Raul's tall white frame trying to seek rescue in the shadows of the verandah, his hand awkwardly half raised in the air defensively. I remember how scared his eyes were, almost bulging from their sockets, his chest rising up and down wildly.

I remember his father magistrate Lewis standing there, too afraid to advance towards my mother, too afraid to do anything at all. I remember him saying, "Think about your child madam. If you kill my son who is going to take care of your child?"

I think magistrate Lewis knew exactly what to say to calm the situation. My mother was never arrested. She left Raul with a strict warning, that she would raise hell itself and bring forth the devil if he came near me again.

However, magistrate Lewis made sure my mother paid for that day on the veranda. When Paul Moses stood before him in the courthouse, he took his revenge.

Everyone knew about Raul Lewis. Everyone knew about his father's influence in the law and politics of Grenada. Magistrate Lewis was from a long standing generation of deputation sent from Britain and thus represented the eyes and the voice of our colonial mother on our small island. The Lewis family had money. They had lands and above all they had power.

Raul Lewis was what one would call devilishly handsome. He had wide blue eyes and a saintly smile, but he was a fiend in disguise. I was twelve years old when he committed his vile act. I remember hearing stories of him growing up; like that time he touched Miss Mildred's daughter who was sent to deliver fresh cow's milk to their house; and that other time he was caught peeping at some young girls bathing in the river. I heard many stories like that, but nothing was ever done because of his family's influence. My mother was the first and only person who ever stood up to him. People were too afraid to cross paths with magistrate Lewis.

Two years after the event with my mother, Raul Lewis was sent to England. The butcher's wife who worked for the family informed my mother that Raul had taken advantage of a young girl and that his father had paid the family handsomely to keep quiet. The girl's father was a known drunkard who was all too happy to fill his pockets with the hushed settlement. I never knew what became of the girl or who she was even, but Raul was sent to England to get married. I guess his father thought marriage could cure him.

A place where children are not safe should never be called a community.

16.

Celeste

Celeste was the daughter of Mr. Ben, the butcher. Everyone loved Celeste. She had a petite frame and a squeaky voice and a mischievous grin was always painted on her face, but it was her sprightly and humerous nature that made her stand out. She could make anyone laugh, even those older than her.

I was four forms ahead of Celeste in school but knew her well. She spent a lot of time in my house because our mothers were friends. Sometimes her mother paid me to look after her when my mother was not at home to do so. Celeste and I would always spend the money on conkies. I remember her little fingers diligently unpeeling the cooked banana leaf and staring happily at the sticky content. I remember her laughing and licking the leaf, even after the sweet-flavoured corn meal had disappeared. She would then run around with the leaf on her head, while dancing and making funny faces and we would laugh to our hearts' content.

One rainy evening her mother came knocking on our door, desperately asking if we had seen Celeste. It was unusual of her to be late from school. The next day Celeste's lifeless body was found inside the old abandoned house we often passed by on our way home from school. She must have gone there to seek shelter from the heavy rains that evening.

She was still wearing her school uniform. It seemed as if she had fought her killer hard. Her hair was dishevelled, her shirt was torn and rumpled, and her school skirt was nowhere to be found; and in the far corner of the delapidated room, was a single black shoe. She must have thrown it at him, or it was pulled off while being dragged against her will. Looking down at her lifeless body took me back to Susan, but this time it was another mother clutching her child. The butcher, unlike his wife did not cry. He buried himself in his work.

Not all those who stand accused are guilty. And at the end of the day the universe knows when her books are unbalanced.

17.
Karl

Karl, the village reject, was charged and hanged for the rape and murder of Celeste. His stick-like almost skeletal frame was too light for his neck to break on the plunging impact. He had struggled in mid-air for what seemed as forever, gagging desperately and kicking wildly as life slowly dripped from his body.

Those who witnessed his execution wished they could erase the haunting image of his lifeless body from their minds. I heard the story from my brother who knew one of the men present at the hanging. Karl had suffered throughout his life and even in his final moment. The doctor who was present had to be hospitalized, after being forced to administer a humane procedure that would stop Karl from suffering as he struggled with the rope. The whole island was left in utter sadness for we all knew an innocent man was put to death. Karl was innocent.

Two days before the crime, Raul Lewis had returned to Grenada with his beautiful wife. The old abandoned house was his favourite hunting ground since he knew school girls often took that route on a daily basis. It was at that same place he had exposed himself to me.

Karl was hanged for the evil crime of Raul. The magistrate who delivered the sentence was magistrate Lewis. At his trial and sentencing, Karl had professed his innocence but he was no match for well-formed evidence.

As he was carried off in chains he smiled and warned, "God eyes ent close. God eyes ent close at all." My mother said it was a good thing his parents were both dead and he had no family to see his final end, but Karl was my family. I knew him well. We often swapped stories. He was even a friend of Ole Mary's. He was a kind gentle soul who had been dealt a card of misfortune. His parents had died in a house fire. Thereafter he had wandered the streets, sleeping below people's houses and in abandoned buildings. I was overwhelmed with mixed emotions — both anger and sadness wrestled — wrestled with my sanity.

Say your truth without fear. If you are not fighting for the truth, then what are you fighting for?

18.

The Rebellion

I sat there, watching the hypocrisy and sheer evil that plagued our society. The church was filled with people but a murderer and rapist was walking free. Everyone knew that Karl was innocent of the crime. All of them knew an innocent man was hanged for a crime he did not commit and could not have committed. However everyone went along with the mendacity, out of cowardice—out of fear of magistrate Lewis.

I wanted so badly to stand up and call them out, to tell them that by sitting in silence they were all guilty of the crime. I wanted to scream. I wanted to rip away the lies that covered their faces but I remained calm, stifling my emotions, my candour, for the sake of Celeste.

Celeste, my friend, my sister, my comrade in arms, who was now lying in a coffin in front of me. Celeste, who once threw a dead frog on her mother and laughed her heart out when her mother started jumping and screaming. Celeste, who had eaten all her mother's plum stew from the jar and replaced the missing plums with small stones. Celeste, the girl who loved helping others. Celeste, who used to strip naked and jump in the river shouting, "What you have, I have too." Celeste, who used to follow me around because she saw me as a big sister. My Celeste! I had loved her with every inch of my soul.

She was buried on a Friday and our school was given a whole day off to attend the funeral and to mourn. On the Sunday, my gang and I met up as we always did after Sunday school. Our gang was named after our heroine Mary Magdalene. We had all taken an oath to protect each other. Celeste was the youngest member of our gang and she was going to be avenged.

On Monday morning our form mistress entered our form to take the attendance, but this time no one stood up to extend the customary greetings that were expected from us. Utter surprise and anger ran across her face, but she remained quiet. She then started calling our names one by one, as an indication that we should stand and greet her, but no one complied. We all sat there glaring at her, waiting for her to make the next move we so much anticipated.

She then rushed out and came back with three teachers and the principal. Miss Jacob looked directly at me and said, "Stop this, because it will not end well for you this time."

"Her name was Celeste Barry and you and I both know that her rapist and murderer still walks the street," I responded defiantly.

She then walked up to me and grabbed me by the hand, as if to forcefully drag me out of the classroom. I spun her around and she fell to the floor and that was when it started—teachers versus students, young women against a system that offered them no protection. They fought us hard and we fought back harder, using anything our hands found to vent out our anger. We pulled hair as weeds from a garden. We bit like rabid dogs. We threw tables and chairs like grenades. We tore at the plaques on the walls. We kicked. We screamed.

Then we took to the streets, chanting at the top of our lungs, "Justice for Celeste! Justice for Celeste!" Here we were shouting at the top of our voices, on the very streets we once walked in silence, too afraid to be deemed as 'bad girls'. I was at the front of the line. We were one, screaming in unison—bloodied, torn school shirts, dishevelled hair, broken lips, swollen eyes, but still we found the strength to shout, "Justice for Celeste!"

When we got to the courthouse we shouted even louder, "Justice for Celeste! Mary Magdalene! Justice for Celeste! Mary Magelene!" we screamed.

We threw stone after stone at the building until we could throw no more. We broke windows. We hammered at the door to let us in but the planks of solid mahogany remained firm. We would have certainly burned it to the ground if given the chance.

Then they came. In their hands they held batons, but we did not fear their batons. How many times had we seen far worse—lack of voice, lack of choice, no freedom

144

to be, to live, our very lives dictated, our voice choked until it became no more. Our souls joined in unison as we laughed at their batons—laughed because we had seen far worse.

There we were, hands locked together. We did not care about skin color, or hair texture, or social status, for we had burnt it all—all of society's walls and barriers. We were one soul, screaming to be free from oppression and hypocrisy. We screamed for all the women that went before us. We screamed and brought forth Shango priestesses and old Obeah women from their graves. We screamed and brought forth the spirits of the women who had died during the middle passage; those who died in bondage; those who died fighting to be free. We screamed for all the souls denied a body, denied a chance to suckle on their mother's breast, because society would judge and chatize them, like their mothers. We screamed and brought forth the souls of the Kalingo women who were raped, murdered and buried in unmarked graves. We screamed for the blistered hands of the women who toiled on the nutmeg and cocoa plantations and were still given less—their hands knotted, tired and old with stony corns and blisters. We screamed at the irony of it all—that we, the givers of life, would be barred from life.

What did we care about their batons? We laughed at their batons—laughed because we had seen far worse.

On that day, all thirty-one of us were taken into police custody—but even the iron bars could not contain us, as we continued our protest. "Justice for Celeste! Mary Magdalene !" we wailed.

We were let off with a strict warning. Maybe it was because some of the girls had affluent parents. Maybe it was because hypocrisy was trembling and was afraid for once on the island of Grenada.

The universe has a balance. When things are unbalanced, order must be restored.

19.

Post Rebellion

One day while sitting outside with Ole Mary by her chicken coup, just staring at nothing and at everything at the same time, a woman showed up. She had travelled all the way from the countryside to see Ole Mary for a special portion and some prayers. She believed her womb was cursed—her mother-in-law's doing.

She gave Ole Mary the chicken that she had carried from her home, carefully tucked below her arm and in return Ole Mary gave her a portion to drink and an ointment to rub at nights.

When the woman left I said to Ole Mary, "Father Stephen said you are the devil and you are going to hell."

Ole Mary looked at me and bursted out laughing, which showed off her perfect white pearly teeth. They were abnormally white as if they did not belong to her. She then contested, "Which hell? His hell, his white hell, the one that justifies years of plantation slavery; the rape of the black woman; black murders; the oppression; is that the hell he speaks of?"

"He said you are an Obeah woman," I continued.

"What is Obeah child? I know how to use herbs and I understand the universe and the universe speaks of two things; anything you throw out into the universe will find its way back to you. So one should taste his words and carefully weigh his actions because it shall be returned tenfold. The second is, do not to be filled with arrogance and pride. Man is borrowed and one day all things borrowed shall be returned to its maker, and he shall ask you about your actions towards all of his children—all of his children, not some, not just those you like."

She then went on to say, "I am proud of knowing what I know and what I know comes all the way from where my people came from, from where we were stolen and brought here in chains—to be slaves. They want you to hate your African identity; for a people lacking in knowledge of self is lost. From the day they stole us and brought us here, they have been trying to break us and break us they have, by teaching us to hate ourselves, but they only broke some of us, some of us remained whole and alive. If my beliefs are so evil and I am so evil, you think that the priest and all his other white friends would still be alive today, after all the wicked things they did to us in slavery days and are still doing today? You are a bright girl, think!"

"He said you have a 'bad book' that you read from," I insisted.

She then angrily exclaimed, "Look child, my book contains prayers of all sorts and herbal remedies that have been passed down from generation to generation—first by word of mouth, then on paper. Just because I know how to use herbs, that does not make me evil. Just because I am a woman who will never embrace fear of any sort, that does not render me evil. Just because I am a woman who knows how to pray that does not render me evil. My eyes are blue because my mammy's eyes were blue, but she did not get those eyes from her mammy; she got it from her daddy. She got it from her blue-eyed father, magistrate Lewis' father. He forced those blue eyes onto her. You see, his father and his father before him were exactly as Raul, nasty and vile and don't think magistrate Lewis is any different. So many young girls he has used and forced in to silence because he thinks he is above it all, but we shall see. We shall see."

They say many things about dreams and dreams say many things to them.

20.

The Dream

Later that night I dreamt I was dancing to the sound of drums. My body moved fast enough to match each beat, my heart and the trance-like rhythm became one, sweat poured off my forehead, my white dress flew in all directions. In my neck hung a brown beaded necklace, made from cotton string and 'donkey eye' seeds and around my ankles were a matching pair. I was happy for the drums made me feel free.

Then all of a sudden the drums stopped and I was surrounded by many people dressed in white, both males and females. A man dressed in a torn white pants came up to me. He offered me a warm smile and wrote something in the dirt in front of me. It read 'Toussaint Louverture'. Then an old woman came up to me and did the same, it read 'Nanny'. Then another man came up and did the same, it read 'Samuel Sharpe'. In the end there were many names written on the ground before me; Bussa of Barbados, Kofi of Berbice, Quamina of Demerara and many more names. I knew each and every one of those names, for they had all fought for justice. Finally they all formed a tight circle around me and chanted a name I had never heard before—a name I could not remember when I woke up.

When I told Ole Mary about my strange dream she said, "That was no dream and the name will come to you when you meet him."

Every like has its alike. When you find your alike, the mysteries of life and its events will show its face and worries will float out the window. The heart knows the trail to the divine and all things divine. Love is divine.

21.
Amir Jallow

At first I thought him a peculiar being. On the days I went with my mother to the market to sell, I would see him at his mother's side awaiting the next customer or already attending to one. The thing that stood out the most about him was his demeanour. He was quiet and oddly mysterious in my child-like eyes.

As I grew older I found myself noticing more of him — like the silkiness of his smooth black-blue skin; like his almond shaped eyes and his long eye lashes; his piercing gaze; like the way he stood upright and bold in a king-like manner; like the way his voice rumbled like a valley's river — deep, determined and commanding.

Then one day he stopped coming to the market. I later found out he had moved to the island of Dominica with his uncle to learn the trade of boat building. I was heartbroken and eventually gave up all thoughts of ever seeing him again. Then one day while sitting by the river, I noticed a figure in the basin further down from where I was perched. It was Amir. For what reason I quickly bolted from where I was sitting, I cannot say. I remember running all the way to my house as if someone was after me.

Thereafter, I would see him from 'time to time', sometimes on the beach with the older boat builders or at the market with his mother. Then finally one day life handed us a reason to speak and an introduction was made. A regular customer of his mother wanted green plantains, and so he was instructed by his mother, to escort the customer to our booth, since my mother was known for her fair prices.

I remember him greeting us with '*Asalaam Alaikum*', instead of the regular 'hello'. He then politely nodded to my mother and me and calmly explained that the customer wanted green plantains.

My mother who was familiar with his family then quickly introduced us with a big smile on her face and said, "Ah Amir and how nice to see you today! Of course you remember my daughter Mary, right?"

He then answered, "Yes I remember Mary. She seems to have a great love for books. She is always reading."

"Yes, she loves reading and writing. She wants to be a lawyer someday. She is awaiting some confirmation," my mother continued.

"Ah," he said, raising his thick eyebrows and smiling, "a woman should be versed on all matters for it is women who raise nations. Plus this place needs one of our own to take care of our people."

At that moment I chuckled nervously, ignoring the fact that my mother and Amir were both speaking about me as if I was not present. On leaving he then said goodbye to me directly. I could not help but notice the sly smile on my mother's face. She held her smile until his tall slender frame disappeared among the hustle and bustle of the marketplace.

On that night I caught myself smiling uncontrollably just before I fell asleep. How did he know I liked reading? My heart tickled with a warm delight as I remembered the highlight of my day.

Two Sundays after, my mother took it upon herself to invite Amir and his family to dinner, and it was there I got the opportunity to talk to him as our parents were busy chit-chatting. However, ever so often I would notice our mothers eyeing us in a knowing, approving way.

I knew a little bit about Islam from Mr. Bishop. He had taught me that Islam was one of the religions brought over to the Caribbean by Africans who were stolen from their homeland. Like all other religions that crossed over the sea, it was practised in secrecy on the plantations, away from the watchful eyes of 'massa', since it was not permitted and thus punishable by beatings, maimings and even death. I knew that Muslims had to pray five compulsory prayers; that they did not eat pork and their religion was a monotheistic one. So when Amir and his family excused themselves to say the *Asr* prayer after their meal, the act itself was not new or bizarre to me.

In a later conversation, he told me that his passion was farming. He said that before anything, men should strive to be farmers and that the soil had thus far taught him compassion, discipline and patience.

I was intrigued not only by his humility and words but also by his thick accent. The manner in which he pronounced certain words gave away the truth, that the English language was not his most familiar tongue although he was Grenadian born. Later on I would hear him speak a language called Walof. It was a magical experience hearing this language for the first time; almost captivating, as if it was the key my soul had been waiting for to unlock it. Time would show us that we had many things in common; one of them being a shared passion for reading and writing. Time would also test us—time would grow my wings and time would cement his roots further, but a coin has two sides. Does it not?

That was Amir Jallow and I, inseparable.

We can't leave with any of it but yet we still fight to acquire so much of it. The idea of living is not about the possession of material things and showing off, it is about rich memories, compassion, family and falling in love. But these things only become clearer as we walk inwards to greet our true selves, our souls. Greet your souls. Begin the long walk.

22.

New Journey

When I turned eighteen I legally inherited half of the wealth my father had left behind. The other half was given to my brother and his mother. My brother donated all of his inheritance to the church. We kept in contact over the years, and developed a relationship from the meagre strips the past had left us.

At age nineteen, I had more than enough money to finance my education and live a comfortable life, and with the help of my brother and my excellent grades, I was accepted to an esteemed law school in England.

As I said goodbye to my beloved island, to my family, to Amir Jallow, and to Ole Mary, my heart was overflowing with joy and sadness at the same time, for I was about to embark on a new journey, but that meant leaving behind everything and everyone I had grown to love.

In my ear, Ole Mary had whispered, "Everything happens for a reason. My womb can bear no Mary. This is the end of my lineage, but there is hope. You are the hope.

A revolution is coming and an Ole Mary will be needed. A revolution is coming, this island will need an Ole Mary."

Epilogue

I was in form 5 when he appeared at our door steps. He came looking for Paul. He returned the next day with fruits. The following day he came again and offered to cut the grass that was starting to grow tall outside of our house. I was all too delighted to have someone do my chores free of charge, and as my mother and I kept him company and satisfied with freshly made lemon juice, I could not help but notice the way his eyes followed my mother. It was uncomfortable to observe but it warmed my heart.

Our house was no longer the little green house with the mustard coloured front door from my childhood. It was now bigger and more spacious. My mother had made some extensions—five rooms were added, each with its own entrance. She rented these rooms to those passing by and seeking short term housing or a night's lodging. She no longer washed and ironed for a living and she eventually gave up gardening and leased her ten acres of land to a friend.

On the fourth day, he asked for lodging. It was now quite obvious he fancied my mother and it seemed that she fancied him also. She started wearing her prettier dresses. She started laughing more and strangely enough, we grew closer. Some parts of me had not forgiven her but I made peace with the past. Lloyd had brought fresh light into our lives.

He was a gifted musician. He knew Paul from Her Majesty's Prison. Lloyd had struck an Indian overseer to near death in vexation in response to being called a 'nigger'. On the day he asked my mother to marry him, he made a big scene by inviting all the neighbours. My mother could not refuse.

As luck would have it, Lloyd was an excellent chef also. Together they opened a small food parlour next to our home. His food attracted customers from far and wide. Soon after, they bought a motor vehicle and became the talk of the village.

Liz, my dear old friend, became a teacher and she was a brilliant and loving one. Ruth, the friend I had once given to the wind also become a teacher, and later became one of the most famous women on our island.

A year after I left Grenada Mrs. McMillan went mad. I heard it from my sister Paulette, who heard it from one of the McMillans' maids. She said just like that Mrs. McMillan started screaming and pulling at her hair and dress, shouting, "Get them off! Get them off!" Another time she pointed to the doorway and said, "Look at him there. He come to take my soul. *Aidez moi! Aidez Moi!*

Aidez moi! Il est la! Papa Legba est la! Il est la! Il vient pour moi!" she regularly screamed in French. In the end she was admitted to the institution for the mentally insane where she lived out the rest of her days.

The moment I learnt about Mrs. McMillan's plight, I remembered something Ole Mary had said, "When Papa Legba comes for their soul, they will see their deeds and he cares not for repentance."

Raul and his father went out to sea to fish one lovely Sunday evening and they were never seen again. Candles were lit for them to return safely home, but the seas screamed, 'When Papa Legba comes for their soul, they will see their deeds and he cares not for repentance'.

Kissandra Smith

Life

If I test you not, how will you transcend human boundaries and ambitions and find your way back to the land of souls, where you will meet your maker, as he is our maker.

The Rebellion of Mary Magdalene

Ole Mary

Life has given me many dark cards but I refused to play with them. Instead I created my own stack of cards to play with, filled with light. Sometimes we curse ourselves.

Hazel

Tell him you love him. Tell her you love her. Tell! Tell! Tell! Then runaway together if you must.

The Rebellion of Mary Magdalene

Paul McMillan Sr.

The treasures of the heart are far greater than any treasure seen by the eyes of men.

Paul McMillan Jr.

Courage and honesty make a man. Lies and lack of courage make him a wild beast.

Ruth

Oh beautiful one, you must not let them steal your soul also. You are the rising phoenix. Born of fire and flame and that too is beautiful.

Paul Moses

Whatever you do for or do to another human being, you do for or to your own self.

The Rebellion of Mary Magdalene

Paulette Moses

Do we say accept the past, because the reality is, we cannot change it? Or do we really accept our past mistakes and follies as the fuel for our growth?

You are not abnormal for having regrets. You are allowed to have them, but don't water them to the point that they become your poison.

I regret many things, but I chose to use them for growth. The idea is to fashion them into weapons of love, wisdom and compassion.

Mary Moses

If you don't know my madness then you don't know me at all.
If you have not done anything crazy with me in which we laughed about it after, then you have not done anything with me.

If you still think I belong within the different parentheses that you have created for me, then you are far from my truth.

If you still think I should be normal, your normal that is, then you are indeed abnormal.

Cheers to the people who redefine definitions, push the borders of brackets, the misfits, the semi colons, the ellipses, the rebellious, the Ole Marys, those who fan the flames of love and madness, only to dance in the fire, only to be reborn again and again.

The Rebellion of Mary Magdalene

Liz Bishop

I do not fear death. I fear the life of a simple mind that sorely awaits the new dawn, without knowing the meaning of the new dawn.

Kissandra Smith

Mr. Bishop

Fear not the barrel of a gun, for it was made by a man and it is held by a man. Let your truth be your amour. And be weary of he who aspires to become a leader, for it is the universe which bestows such an honour; and it is rebellion that enacts change, continuance of an oppressive regime and ideologies will never alter the tides of time.

Karl

Compassion is the heart of humanity. If you have none for the vulnerable then I fear you are not human. You are not even a soul. You are a cage filled with nothing.

Celeste

Your silence is the problem.

The End

‹AMERHOGNE
PRESS

Printed in Great Britain
by Amazon